ROBERT

ARCHER'S DYNASTY BOOK 3

KATHI S. BARTON

This is a work of fiction. Names, characters, places, and incidents are products of the author's imagination or are used fictitiously and are not to be construed as real. Any resemblance to actual events, locations, organizations, or persons, living or dead, is entirely coincidental.

World Castle Publishing, LLC
Pensacola, Florida
Copyright © Kathi S. Barton 2022
Hardcover ISBN: 9798356503054
Paperback ISBN: 9781958336748
eBook ISBN: 9781958336755
First Edition World Castle Publishing, LLC, October 6, 2022
http://www.worldcastlepublishing.com
Licensing Notes
Cover: Karen Fuller
Editor: Karen Fuller

Prologue

Robert watched the men as they worked on the house he knew Heather and Peter were going to live in. He was hoping he could convince them to let him purchase the other house from them when it was finished.

The workers were doing all sorts of things he'd never thought of before that were needed to bring a house back to life, like hanging drywall. The way they put a strip of some kind of paper tape over the seams to what he assumed was to hide them. He was just about to move to another part of the house to watch more work going on when Mr. Taylor, the foreman, sat down beside him.

"You're here to make sure we're doing a good

job?" Robert was shocked by the question. "You're making my people nervous, Mr. Archer. If you're going to be spying on us, the least you could do was to inform me that you're doing that."

"Oh. No. That's not it at all. I didn't think that it would— You see, I'm an attorney. Not that it has anything to do with me being here. But I don't want to do that anymore. Not at all." Mr. Taylor nodded. "I'll start from the beginning. I don't like being an attorney. I don't know that I ever did. So I'm looking for, I don't know, something to occupy my mind and body. I was watching your workers because I've been thinking I'd like to give something like this a shot. You know, it's physical. Mentally challenging. I mean, to watch how your people can hang the boards there and not have to second guess if it's going to stay there or even fit. I was trying to decide if this was something I'd like to try."

Mr. Taylor took the notebook that he'd offered to him. As he read over the pages he'd been taking notes on from different jobs on the site, he handed it back to him and sat there for several minutes. It was all he could do not to beg him not to turn him away.

"Come with me." As he walked up the stairs to the third floor, he introduced him to the elderly man working there. "This is Bingo. Don't ask how he got the name. Bingo, this is Robert. He's going to be working with you today. He's a greenhorn, so don't be making him do all your work while you supervise. He's got it in his head that he wants to work in renovations like this house."

Bingo took his hand when he offered it. "He thinks on account of me being old, that I don't know a thing or two. You're an Archer. I noticed he didn't give a last name, but I've been around the block a time or two, so I know what's what more than he does. You're a lawyer, ain't you?"

"Yes. I was, I guess you could say. I'll still work if I'm needed, but I'm bored with it. At least for now. I need something to keep me out of trouble." Bingo laughed. "My mom said that if I didn't find something to do soon, she was going to murder me. I doubt it would come to that, but she doesn't have anything around the house for me to move or to help her clean."

Bingo laughed again. It was like listening to a braying jackass, as his grandda would say. But it was also a good sound like he really meant the humor of it. When he told him to come with him, he once again found himself following someone. But this time, he was handed a diagram of what the floor was to look like when it was finished.

"That there is called tile rejuvenation. Not thinking you're stupid or nothing, but that's what I call it. The design there, it's what was on the floor before some fool covered it with carpet, it looked like. What I've been doing, and you're going to do now, is take that there scraper thing and peel back all that stuck crap over it and bring out the tile. Not hard, not if you're a young man such as yourself, but it's hard on an old man like me. Just be careful, because some of them tiles is broken, and it'll cut you faster than a sharp blade will. And it's nasty. Being in a bathroom all this time, it's bound to have some nasty turd stuff on it." Robert started to laugh but could see the man was serious. "Now the tricky part of this is going to be when you get there by the terlit. We'll take it out of here if you'd not mind helping me. We're going to be real careful like with it on account of it being old, and it's a good flusher."

It took Robert a second or two to realize he was talking about the toilet. Terlit? It was a word he'd never heard before, but he got it. Watching Bingo as he showed him around the other things he was going to be working on, Robert realized how excited he was to be doing this. He also had a feeling that tomorrow he was going to be sore. He'd not done real physical work in a long time. And going to the gym three times a week wasn't going to even be close to the work he was going to be doing today.

Removing the toilet, or terlit as Bingo kept calling it, wasn't as difficult as he thought it would be. It was heavy as hell, weighing about a hundred pounds. But it was slippery and awkward to maneuver out of the room. Robert was proud of himself when he got it into the bedroom that this room was attached to.

After removing the pedestal sink and the leg of it, the entire bathroom looked a good deal larger. However, he wasn't sure what they were going to do with the claw footed bathtub. He wondered how they were going to get it out because it was cast iron, Bingo said.

"Waiting on word about that from your brother. Don't suppose you could call him or his missus for me? Sure would be nice to know if we gotta bust out a wall or two to get that sucker out of here. Thing must weight upwards to four hundred pounds or so." He said he'd call him now. "Tell him it can be redone with new enamel coating for about what it'll cost for a new tub."

He was asked to call Heather, as Peter hadn't any idea what she wanted to do. Robert did know that Peter and Heather were going to be living in this house and was a little jealous that they were having so much fun. Robert wondered briefly if he had someone out there that he could love. When Heather answered the phone, he told her what he was doing and why he was calling her.

"Is this the bathroom on the third floor? The one with the wraparound shower curtain that's blue?" He told her it was. "Mr. Taylor told me it had tile under the carpet. Please tell me that's what you're— Wait, what are you doing there?"

"I've decided I need something to do. While I don't need to work for financial gain, I do need to work to keep me from being arrested for sitting outside the different shops around town to browse around more. I've seen about everything there is to see in the shops, just so you're aware." She asked him if he was the go-between. "No. I'm working on the job site if they allow it. Bingo is showing me how to clean the tile under the carpet in there, but the tub is the issue. If it were me, I'd save the tub and the tile. From what I can see of it now, it's beautiful. And the design that was laid here is magnificent. The tile is hexagon-shaped and about an inch and a half across. They alternate between white and blue, with the blue making a kind of hexagon circle around the white. Bingo said there might be a few broken tiles, but I'm betting they can be replaced if necessary."

"You convinced me. Keep them both. I do love the claw-footed tub, so that was going to stay regardless. So I'll find someone to go in and fix it up so it will be all right for us to use. I'm so excited. You go ahead and figure out what it will cost to replace tiles if I need to. Thank you, Robert. I think having you there will help me in being able to settle things like that. Mr. Taylor would give me details but not tell me how lovely it'd look or give me the design you described so well. Thank you bunches." He asked her about the other house. "You want it? I would love to see it go to someone else in the family. It's a big house. Are you looking to fill it anytime soon?"

"Someday." He looked at Bingo and told him she wanted the tub. He laughed when the man did a little gig. It was the perfect word for the dance the man did around the room. "I have to go, Heather. I'll talk to you when I get off work."

Robert had the floor done before lunch. Well, not finished, but he had all the sticky carpet material taken off. While it had been enjoyable work — being entertained by Bingo fun — it was hard, and the muscles across his shoulders and neck were about as strained as he'd ever felt before. However, he was satisfied about the work he'd done and couldn't wait to get more of the work finished up.

Setting to work to clean the tile with a scrub brush and detergent, he reached as far beneath the tub as he could reach. Bingo was going to help him move it a little when he got done with this part of the floor so it would be evenly matched in cleanliness.

Robert was so engrossed in what he was doing that he jerked away from someone touching his back and slammed his head against the tub. When he woke up, he thought he'd fallen asleep on his couch. Trying to sit up, he was shoved back to something hard beneath him and realized he was still in the bathroom, on the floor. It occurred to him that someone was talking about him.

"How the hell am I supposed to know, Grandda? All I did was try and get his attention like you told me to. Christ, you should have seen all that blood." A mumbling sound, then laughter, made him realize that Bingo was who the woman was talking to. He reached up to pull whatever she had on his face down. The woman turned to him. "Look. You take this cloth off your face again, and I'm going to make you hurt worse than you are now. Do

I make myself clear? I'm waiting on one of the drywall jockeys to bring me my bag. How would you rate your pain on a scale of one to ten?"

"It's building up to about a fifty right now. Who are you? And for that matter, what sort of bag are you looking for? You planning on staying the night here?" He was addled, he knew that, but the look she gave him made him think she wasn't amused by him. "I don't know who you are or why you were to get in touch with me. I've got a headache to end all— Is that my blood?"

"Gee, is it? I don't know. Let me wipe at your forehead that is going to more than likely need about thirty stitches from you slamming your fool head up against a tub that more than likely weighs more than the two of us together. You moron. Why didn't you just turn like a normal person?" He told her she'd startled him. "Next time I go into a bathroom that someone is working in with twenty other people around, I'll try my best to make a great deal of noise so as not to startle you. Leave. The. Fucking. Rag. On. Your. Face."

If he wasn't in so much pain at the moment, he would have laughed. However, he might have been in worse shape if he had. The woman wasn't in the best of humor, so he laid there, thinking of all the things he could be doing right now instead of being—

"My brother, Darrel, is a doctor. Not that you have to call him or anything, but…we might want to call my brother Peter. This is his house." He started to reach for the cloth but decided he didn't want to rile her again. "If you could please call my brother, his name is Peter, and it's in my phone."

He felt his phone being taken from his pocket. Telling her the passcode to open it up, he waited while she made the call. The pain was making him sick right now, and he wasn't sure how close he was to begging, literally begging, for something for pain.

"Hey. My name is Doctor Elizabeth Monroe. I'd like to speak to Peter. I didn't catch his last name, so I hope—" He told her what his last name was. "Peter Archer. I'm here with his brother Robert."

Robert wanted to peek at her. She most certainly was nicer than she'd been to him. And he was hurt. He heard her also say thanks to someone else in the room with them. Then the sound of a zipper being used.

"You allergic to anything?" He took a second to realize she was talking to him, and that earned him a poke in the ribs. "Are you allergic to anything?"

"No. And if that is something for pain, I will

gladly take as much as you can give me. I'm cross-eyed with pain right now." His T-shirt was pulled up over his arm, and he felt the coolness of something wiping over his skin. As soon as she told him he was going to feel a pinch, the needle entered him, along with some nice drugs. "Thank goodness."

The next time he was aware, Robert could hear people talking around him — his mom, then his sister-in-law. He didn't know which one it was right now, but he knew it was one of them. Reaching up slowly to pull away whatever was on his face this time, someone touched their hand to his.

"Don't do that. If you do, that doctor is going to come back in here and rip you a new ass. Again." He asked Peter where he was. "Emergency room. You've been here about an hour. Darrel is talking to Elizabeth now on what happened and how they're going to treat you. When you hit your head on that tub, you did some serious damage to your pretty face. Like you have an eruption on your forehead that is going to need some serious stitches in it. Let me describe it for you. It's like you hit the hard surface in the middle. But then the wound split off in about four or five directions from there. Also, you have a concussion, which anyone would figure out. You can have something more for pain should you want it."

"Seriously? Just, I don't know. Don't describe things to me so graphically. I'm all right with the pain right now, but I can feel it building up again. Peter, I'm so sorry about this." He asked him why he was sorry. "I think I might have gotten blood all over your tile. I don't know enough about it to tell you if there is a lot or not, but I'm reasonably sure it's going to stain it."

"I'm just happy you're awake and seem to know what's going on, little brother. And that you're going to heal. You could have really hurt yourself." He thought he had but let it go. "The doctor is coming in again. Just behave and don't piss her off again. She is delightful to watch trying to deal with her anger, but I don't want her to kill you. She's intense."

That was an understatement if he'd ever heard one. While he tried not to sob like a little baby with the pain, he realized he was going into surgery. After asking a couple of questions about it, he asked for pain meds.

"You'll be out in about ten minutes. Will you be able to wait that long?" He told Elizabeth he wasn't sure he could. "I can give you a little of what I'm going to have you put under with, and that won't hurt you during surgery. Just hang on a moment while I get it for you. Robert, I'm really sorry I hurt you."

He said her name to tell her it hadn't been her fault when Peter told him she'd gone. Then seconds later, he felt the pain being dulled, and he let himself ride on that. Christ, he was going to be a mess when he woke up. He knew it.

~*~

Elizabeth was used to stitching people up. She'd been an ER doctor for the last five years. However, she'd caused this wound to this man, and his family had been nothing but nice to her. She, however, felt like shit about it. Darrel, who was assisting her so that he could vouch for her abilities to work in the hospital, asked her if she was all right to begin.

"I'm responsible for this. He was working, and I startled him to the point where he jumped. I feel just horrible." Darrel told her Robert wouldn't feel that way. "No. Then after he woke up, I was nasty to him again. I'm not sure I can see him again after this."

"You mean after the surgery or just in general?" She wasn't sure what he meant, so she asked him. "I mean, would you like to see him on a personal level, or just as follow up after this? He's a great man, if you mean personally. As for the follow-up? Well, I can do that, but I think you're going to regret it. Robert will as well. I mean, it could go nowhere, but if you were to ask me, I think you'll miss someone great in your life as a friend if you forgo seeing him in either capacity."

"He'll make me feel bad about hurting him." Darrel just laughed. "I don't think this is the least bit funny. Even if there was to be something romantic — I'm not saying that's what I want — but even if there was, I'm sure he'd hold what I did to him over my head for decades to come."

"Nor do I think this is funny. As for him holding it over your head, you'd never allow that. You'd be all over his ass, or you'd leave. You strike me as a woman who doesn't take shit from anyone. However, I can almost bet that not only will Robert never blame you for anything that happened to him at work, but you can bet he'll take you to task if you were to tell him you hurt him." She asked him how he could be so sure. "He's my brother, for one thing. I'm as sure about his reaction to you and your ideas as I am about you being a good doctor. Secondly, my mom would beat his ass if he even thought about hurting you. Now, how about we get this show on the road and get him fixed up?"

The surgery went well. The reason they had opted to go into the surgical room was so they could make sure nothing had gotten into the wound. The tub, while hard as stone, was old and hadn't been cleaned in some time. After cleaning the wound several times, finding a small piece of enamel in the wound, Elizabeth put tape over it to help with the probable scarring. They'd have to wait a couple of more days to stitch him up, as the swelling was more than it had been before they'd brought him in here.

Checking on him in recovery, Elizabeth was shocked to hear him call out to anyone that was in the room with him. Answering his question about who she was and why she was there, he grabbed her hand like a lifeline. Holding him too, she told him what had happened in the operating room.

"Thank you for taking such good care of me. I know Darrel would have done the same, but he might well have left some kind of carving in my head. Just to make fun of me later." She told him then that she was sorry. "For what? I haven't any idea why you'd think what I did to myself is in any way connected to you, but get that thought out of your head right now. I did this by being so engrossed in cleaning tile that I simply shut out the world around me."

"But if I'd not—" He told her that no one was at fault. "I did startle you. If I'd not, then you wouldn't be here now."

"Elizabeth—can I call you that?" She nodded, then told him he could. His head was bandaged up, so his eyes were covered up as well. "You want to make this up to me? Then you can have dinner with me. I've not had a date in a long time, so I'm not even sure if it's all right for a man to ask a woman. I've been leading a very sheltered life up until now."

"You're a good-looking attorney working with a construction company that my grandda owns, and you've been sheltered? Tug on the other leg, why don't you? That one is long enough." They both laughed, then he moaned in pain. "Don't let the pain get ahead of you, Robert. If you need something for pain, then ask for it."

"I'm enjoying talking to you. But the pain is getting bad again. Will you stay with me until the meds kick in? You more than likely have a lot of things to do, but just for a little while. Please?" She said she would and used the call light to order his medication. As soon as the nurse brought it in, he released her hand. It was the most bereft feeling she'd ever had. "Yes. That's it. I can feel it working."

She stayed with him until she had to go to the bathroom, long after he'd fallen into a deep sleep. Even then, she didn't want to leave. Elizabeth came back in the room for a few more minutes and did something she hadn't ever done to a patient in her life. Kissing him on the mouth, she left the room before someone could tell her she was a fool.

Going back to her grandda's house, she was surprised to see he'd been prepared for her coming in late. Sitting at the kitchen table with him, he handed her a plate of cold sandwiches and carrots. She didn't care for chips, and Elizabeth loved that he had remembered that about her.

"You get him all fixed up?" That was all it took for her to burst into tears. She was so upset her grandda came around the table to hold her. "Honey, I don't know what's upset you about him, but I will have him fired tomorrow morn—"

"No. No, it's not that at all. Grandda, he was super nice to me even though I caused him to be hurt. He was a gentleman and so kind to me about it not being my fault. Robert told me it was entirely his fault for being so— Grandda, I really like this man. I know I've known him for less than a day, and most of that was him being unconscious, but he was nice to me and kind. It's been a long time since anyone has been kind to me that wasn't related to me." Grandda said he liked him as well. "I don't know what I'm to do about this."

"About what? You mean liking him? What's the problem with liking a nice man? Nothing. Are you wondering if he'd like you? He'd be a darn fool not to like you. Even perhaps fall in love with you someday. As for anything else going on in that pretty little head of yours, you can forget that right now. All those Archers are good people, from the elderly man to the youngest one. Why, I'd be as happy as a lark in the summer if you were to attach yourself to someone like that. I'm not saying you have to, but you couldn't do any worse." She said he was putting the cart before the horse. "Perhaps. But I've known you all your life, little bit. And there hasn't ever been a time when you'd been this upset about— You remember that boy in third grade that you put on the straight and narrow? What was his name?"

"Danny Thomas. He pulled on my braids one too many times. When I had enough, I punched him in the face and knocked him on his ass." Grandda laughed and asked her if she remembered getting into trouble. "I was supposed to be suspended for a week, but Grandma went up there with a willow stick and met up with the principal with it in her hand. He started to tell her it was school policy, but she wasn't having it. If I was never afraid of Grandma, that would have been the day I changed my mind. She smacked that stick down on his hands and told him to think about his next words. My goodness, Grandda, I have never in all my life had more respect for her than I did at that moment. She will always be my hero, even though she's been gone for a while."

"I miss that woman every minute of every day. She was the best part of me." Elizabeth said she was for her too. "She could boil you with a look and hug you like you've been gone for years instead of just the day before. I loved her so much. Had it not been for you, honey, I would have gone on with her. She made me a man that I could be proud of."

"When she asked me what I wanted to do with my life, the first thing that popped into my head was nothing. I just wanted to do charity work like she did. But then I thought of her helping that little boy across the street when he fell from the tree. She was so calm and barking orders to his parents. I swear to you, that is the reason I became a doctor. I wanted to be able to help other people when they were at their worst." Grandda used a napkin to blow his nose. "Grandda, we need to do this more often, I think. Talk about Grandma and the things that made her so special to us both. I know I'd love some of the memories you have of her before I came along and messed up your retirement years."

"We were sitting around and being old before you came along. All the money in the world can't do crap for you if you've no one to enjoy it with. And that is exactly what you did when you were brought to us after your parents died. I believe this with all my heart, had you not come along when you did, we'd have been found a month or so after we'd died from boredom, and no one would have given two fiddles about it. No, don't you ever think you messed up our lives, Elizabeth. You gave us a life. Always believe that."

She wiped at her own tears then. Reaching across the table to his hand, she took it into her own. His hands were callused and strong. Nothing like some of the elderly she had taken care of at the hospital that she'd worked at until recently.

"I love you so much, Grandda. Thank you for being just the man you are and making me feel like I was someone very special." He said she'd made that easy. "Well, I love you. And I'm exhausted. I'm going to head up to the bed and get going early in the morning. I need to find me a job before I get into any more trouble."

"You'll make trouble, Elizabeth. You're good at that."

She laughed with him, not sure what he meant by that. But he loved her, and she couldn't have asked for anyone better in her life.

Then she thought of Robert. He was a nice man. Also, he was smart, savvy, and just the sort of person she thought could shake up her life. Getting into bed, she scolded herself for acting like a lovesick puppy and willed herself to sleep. Of course, it didn't work, and she tossed and turned for what felt like hours before she finally gave up and went to her computer to try and read the latest medical journal magazine. Even that didn't work

"Now, what am I supposed to do when a man I barely know is keeping me up at nights, wondering if he is a good kisser or not? Also, what was I thinking in kissing him like that? I wasn't. That was it." Finally giving up on everything she'd planned for herself, Elizabeth got into the shower and decided to start her day. "Stupid man. What the hell was I thinking when I went and kissed him? My life is really screwed up if I'm resorting to kissing strangers when they're sleeping."

Going to the kitchen again, she opened her laptop and began looking for job postings. When her grandda showed up, Elizabeth realized she'd not applied for a single job and couldn't have told anyone what she'd been looking at either. Even her computer got tired of waiting on her and had gone to sleep. Everything was sleeping better than she was.

~*~

Peter pulled out his cell phone when it vibrated. Having a message from Robert was always a good thing.

I went to the doctor today. Christ, she's beautiful, isn't she? This was the first time I saw her clearly. Anyway, they took the bandages off, and the wounds are healing nicely. He messaged him back, asking him if he'd asked Elizabeth out yet. *I did. We're working up to that.*

Peter told him good. Then he saw that he was typing again.

Dinner tonight? With my new girl?

Sure. Steaks on the grill all right with you? I'll have a nice pork chop for my meal, so it'll be a nice meal for me as well. Robert sent back an emoji of happy faces dancing all over the screen. *Good. Pick up dessert and well have a nice evening.*

Putting his phone on the floor beside him, he held Heather in his arms. Nothing could be better than this, he thought. They were all safe, and he was going to be a father. It was then that it hit him.

He was going to be a father.

Peter had always dreamed of having a couple of kids. The right woman hadn't come along until he met Heather. Now not only was he getting his life in order, thankfully, but he was going to have a little one running around. He thought his grandda would be the happiest. He'd been having a good time playing with the kids at Delmar's home.

"He's never treated them any different than he did if they'd been born of his blood." He was startled when Heather spoke. "You talk when you're thinking hard. Did you know that?"

"I used to do it as a kid, but I thought I'd outgrown that. Robert and Elizabeth are coming over for dinner tonight. They're bringing dessert. Are steaks all right with you?" Heather kissed him on the mouth before getting up. Then she helped him up from the floor. "Christ, but that isn't as painful as it was the first time. I think I'm on the mend. What do you think?"

"I think I miss you in the bed with me. I miss having

you hold me around your naked body." He kissed her again. "And that. Quick kisses aren't as satisfying as one might think."

Peter was still laughing as he made his way to the kitchen. The cane was helping him not go too fast, but it was also annoying to remember he needed it. As soon as he entered the kitchen, he felt like he had always felt at his mom's home. The place of gathering. That was what he thought the definition of a kitchen should be.

~*~

Elizabeth didn't mind going to Peter's home. Since she'd been hanging around with Robert, she'd met and come to like all the family. Grandda was enjoying it as well, as he was getting around town more.

"Did you know he didn't file for worker's comp? I expected him to. He *was* hurt on the job. But he told me that since he'd been foolish enough to get himself hurt, he should pay for it." She said she'd talk to him. "Don't, honey. Let him do this. He's a right proud man, and don't embarrass him for a couple of hundred dollars."

Elizabeth was sure it was a good deal more than that, but she let it go. Darrel had told her just that morning that she was approved to work at the hospital. She'd only need to take her boards in Ohio, and that would be it. In the meantime, he was going to shadow her, so she didn't do anything upsetting to the hospital. Today had been a good day for her.

"Do you think they'd mind if I was to invite myself to this dinner thing?" She told her grandda she didn't think anyone would mind. "You ask them. I won't if it's a family thing, but I'd like to talk to Peter a bit. He's a good man, that one. So is Robert."

"Grandda, I'm not family." She didn't like that he waved her off as if it were a done deal that she was a family member. "I'm not. I'm just going there with Robert to have steaks with his family. There isn't anything going on between the two of us."

"If you say so. However, let me ask you something. When was the last time you lit up when you talked about a man? Never that I can remember. Also, he's a good looking man. A good head on his shoulders and money of his own. Couldn't do any worse than that, I'd not think." She told her grandda not to get the wrong idea. "I don't know that I have the wrong idea, child. Even with his eyes covered, that man follows your voice like you're a nice shiny penny, and he's needing it. My goodness, the heat just about comes off him when the two of you are together."

"He's only just seen me today for the first time." He asked her how that had gone. "I had to beg him to stop talking about how beautiful I was so I could have a look at his wounds. You'd think he'd never seen a woman before."

"I'd say he'd not seen a woman as beautiful as you." She felt her cheeks heat up. "Now then, you ask them if I can join their little get-together, and I'll go get gussied up."

Grandda was still laughing when she pulled out her cell phone. The damned man was driving her insane with his speculations. Just last night, he'd been going on about leaving the company he'd owned forever to Robert. Like he'd just take it because of her.

It was Heather that answered the phone. Before she could ask about her grandda coming, she told her what was going on at the house. She was still smiling as Heather went on about the list of things that were driving her crazy at the moment at their new home.

"Living here isn't so bad. I mean, Robert has asked for it, and I don't mind him taking it. Are you going to be all right living here?" She asked her what it would have to do with her. "I don't know, Elizabeth, maybe because you love him? He certainly does look like he's in love with you."

"I don't know how to remark on that. We're just good friends right now." Heather snorted. "Before we get into a heated debate about this, I was talking to my grandda, and he wants to know if it'd be all right for him to join us tonight. He wants to talk to Peter about something. I don't know if this has anything to do with his attorney passing away a few months ago, but it might."

"Sure, the more, the merrier. We're having steaks and baked potatoes. Also, some kind of salad that Peter loves. And Robert is going to be picking up dessert. I haven't any idea what that might entail for him, but I know he is a huge pie lover. I like it too, but Peter told me that Robert will rate a restaurant poorly if they don't have at least one pie choice on their menu." She told her she'd have to remember that. "All right then, we'll be eating around five, I guess. You guys can show up whenever you want. Robert is going to tour the house a little and then make a decision on whether or not he'll take it off our hands."

"Grandda told me a few days ago that he and my dad had done some of the original work on that house. You'll have to talk to him about that too." She said she would. "The house you and Peter are moving into, he said he thought it was built by the first owners. I'm guessing that would be Peter's great-grandparents or something."

"Yes. That would be…this is awesome. I do hope you're going to be coming around a great deal. I'd love to talk to you about all kinds of things." She said she would on the condition that she was allowed to see the things in the barn. "Oh yes. Oh, my goodness, it is the most spectacular place to be when the sun is shining, or not. I was out there yesterday when it started to rain, and the soft breeze made all the smaller pieces chime with the wind. I'm excited to see all the pieces out in the light. We're going to see if any of the rest of the family wants a couple of the pieces to put into their homes. Katie has already asked for a few of them."

"How generous of you and Peter. I don't know what Robert will want, but I'd like to see them. She was quite famous, his grandmother." They talked a bit more about the things in the barn and then decided they'd see if Merce wanted to join them for lunch sometime soon. "I'm working at the hospital until I get to take my tests for Ohio. They're letting me work some to take the pressure off the doctors, so I'll be covering for vacations and such. I love the ER to work in. I think I'd never leave that area if I didn't have to. But covering for doctors means I have to have rounds too. But I'm happy so long as I can stay around here with my grandda. He's all I have left of family."

"Even if you and Robert don't go any further than you are now, we'll still be here for you. And your grandda. However, like I said, he looks at you, and even before he had his bandages removed, he would listen for you to come near him. I'm not pushing, but I don't think you could do any better than having an Archer in your life." Elizabeth admitted to her that she did like him. "Good. That's all I need for now. If you want more, then I'd say go for it."

When they disconnected the call, she felt better for talking to her. Not that she'd been in a bad place, but to talk to someone, another woman, was refreshing. Merce and Heather were a great deal alike in that they'd tell you how it was before you had to ask. Even if you didn't want to know or hear about whatever it was, they'd tell you. She loved that about all the family.

When Robert showed up to get them, he gave her a bouquet of flowers. She couldn't ever in her life remember anyone giving her flowers before that hadn't been related to her. Having them put into a vase that had been her grandma's made them seem more special. Elizabeth handed him a small box as well.

"It's the book we were talking about. I dug out my grandma's copy. It's signed too." He opened it up to the first page and read the inscription. "There are a lot of first editions around here. Some of them aren't of famous people, but Grandma loved to read. She would write reviews for the books too."

"May I kiss you?" Nodding before she knew what kind of kissing he was going to be giving her, she felt herself being drawn to his body like she'd been begging for it all day. When he wrapped his arms around her waist, pulling her flush with his body, Elizabeth looked up at him. "You're beautiful. I know you must get tired of me saying that to you, but I can't help myself. You are far and away the most lovely creature I've ever laid my eyes on."

The kiss was more than she had expected. So much more. His tongue moved along her lips until she allowed him entrance. While his tongue dueled with hers, she felt him press his cock into her soft flesh and moaned. It was as if the nudge of his cock set all kinds of things in motion for them both. Pulling away from her, Robert held her while they both were breathing hard. It was all she could do not to grab him up and take him right there on the living room floor.

"If you touch me right now, I'm going to be in trouble with my family. There won't be any way I can tear myself from you long enough to allow you to undress, much less make it to my family's home. Christ, I was so wrong about you. You're more than any man could have ever dreamed for when he fell in love with a woman." She asked him if he loved her. "I think I have since the first time I woke up in the hospital, and you held my hand. My brothers would have, but I would never have lived it down. You being there was perfect. Like you are. The most magnificently perfect being that has ever been born to this earth."

"You two ready?"

Grandda's timing was either a godsend or a terrible timing. However, she was glad he'd called them both back to earth. When taking her hand into his, Robert kissed her again, and they were out the door. Grandda talked nonstop on the way over, and she wouldn't have been able to tell anyone a single thing he'd said. This must be love, she told herself. Nothing else could feel this good. Nothing.

Chapter 1

Robert was bored out of his mind. If his family didn't leave him alone, he would have to hide from them when they came over. Not that he didn't love them being concerned for him. But he just needed quiet to deal with the things that had been put on his plate the last few days. Mostly it had to do with the beautiful doctor that was seeing to his care.

Elizabeth was the only person that would back off when he asked. His family? They'd push harder thinking; he supposed he was too stupid to do for himself. He told Peter that when he asked him what he was thinking about.

"It's doubtful that they believe that you're stupid.

Stubborn? Yes, that's a given, but then it's like that with our family. But not stupid. They care about you." He grinned at his brother Peter who he was convalescing with today. "However, I don't know if I'd say that to anyone coming over to change my bandages. You've already pissed off enough people today."

"Who? I've done my best to avoid everyone. I can't think of anyone other than you that I could have pissed off today." His brother started listing the names of all the staff in his house. Robert just stared at him. "I didn't piss off your cook. He asked me what I wanted in the way of an omelet, and I told him I didn't like omelets. I like eggs but not messy with all that other crap in them. Who the hell puts mushrooms and cheese in an egg? No one, that's who."

Peter asked him about fried rice. Baiting him, he knew it and would enjoy it as much as he could. But fried rice? Nope. It had mushrooms and other things in it. He pointed out that it was fried rice, not eggs poured over all kinds of fried stuff that no one in their right mind would have in an egg. Peter, who'd been shot twice a week ago, once in the back and once in the leg, was doing his exercises and wouldn't engage with him when he wanted to have a good argument. He called him a wussy.

"Perhaps, but I'm getting better, and all you're doing is nursing a headache. I'm sure that it hurts like hell. It looks like it would. However, now you have two black eyes, a bruise along your cheeks that looks like you took on a cast iron tub and lost. Oh wait, that is what you did." He said that he'd been working and had gotten startled. Peter barely concealed a smile. "You keep telling people that and see what they believe."

Robert didn't care. People would believe what they wanted, but he knew the truth. He had been hurt because he'd been concentrating hard on what he'd been doing. The tile in the bathroom of Peter's home was lovely, and he'd been working hard on getting all the nasty sticky carpet stuff off of them so that they'd shine when they were cleaned up. When Elizabeth, the construction company's owner granddaughter, had come to talk to him, he'd jumped and slammed his head against the tub.

Thinking of Elizabeth, he couldn't help but wonder what she thought of him. She didn't have any trouble telling him off when he was getting sappy, which she called him flirting with her. She had no difficulty telling anyone off when the mood suited her. He enjoyed that about her.

"Peter, what do you and Heather do at the house

alone? I don't mean sex. Just…I don't know. Do you talk about your day? Watch television? Just curious. I've never been around a couple — well, I've not seen a couple alone at home. I'm just wondering what you guys do when we are not bugging you. I'm bored and need something to think about other than my head hurting." He said that they didn't watch all that much television. But they did talk about their day. "I guess since the two of you are in different fields of work, that would make sense. Talk to me, Peter. I'm going nuts here."

"Do you love her?" He didn't even bother asking about whom he was talking to but said he didn't think he was. "The two of you are a good couple together. She's brash and outspoken. You're the opposite of that. Also, this is strange for me to say to my brother, but you shine when she's in the room with you. Like the sun is shining right on you."

"I feel that way as well. Like a bright light is in the room when she is near me. Not that I think I'm in love with her. I think it's a little soon for that. But she's all that and more when we're together." Heather joined them in the living room and asked what they were talking about. After Peter told her, she looked at him. Before she could speak or yell at him, he said first. "We're just discussing falling in love and what a couple does alone at home. Peter asked me if I was in love with Elizabeth. Honestly, I haven't any idea if I am or not. I like her a great deal. But since I've met her, I've been laid up and in pain. She treats me like I'm a baby. Not in a good way either."

"She wouldn't do that if she thought you were a piece of shit, Robert." That stung a little, but he understood what she was saying. "Also, you might not want to hear this, but she's looking for homes in this area. She and her grandda are going to be hanging out together. I'm not sure what that means, but there you have it. Have you seen the house that she grew up in? It's a charming home but not all that large. I think it only has three bedrooms. Aren't you taking the house that we're giving up? I hope so. I can honestly see the two of you living there with many kids. It's being worked on, too, as you know."

"I'm taking it. I love that old home. Also, I've not said anything to anyone else, but Bingo wants me to take his construction company off his hands. He has it in his head that Elizabeth and I are a couple and that I'll be a part of his family soon." Neither of them said a word. "I should be happy that you're not pushing me into anything, but why are you looking at me like that?"

"You might have gotten hurt on your first day at

working construction, Robert, but Bingo told us that in the few hours you were there, you did an amazing job at work. He said that your attention to detail is dead on. Also, he said that you were observant about how the others around you were working." He said that he was only enjoying the job for a bit. "Perhaps, but I think that he's right. You were having a good time at it. And the way you told me about the tile and tub when you called me had me see what you were talking about without being there. You're organized too. Getting a crew working and doing the job correctly."

"Those are things that I've done all my life. It has nothing to do with running a construction company that has been around for several generations." Heather asked him how extended his family had been in business. "That's not the same thing. Construction is nothing like running the Archer money."

"Why not? I mean, don't you want to make money? Don't you already do things that will make it easier to have ready cash when needed? It's all the same, Robert. The only difference is that you'd be in charge rather than having an entire family go through to work." She laughed at him. "You know, I can see you working at construction. You'd be a hands-on sort of boss. I think you'll be well-liked too. I know that I love you."

"I love you too, Heather." And he did, too. She and Peter were perfect together.

Elizabeth showed up a little after five. They would go over the houses he'd had on his list, but first, he would have her take him to his home. It wasn't for her to pick out carpet or anything. Not yet, but he did want her to see the old house so that he could get a feel for how she might like it.

Robert thought he was going down a dangerous path right now. One part of his head figured they could be good friends, but another part worked toward something more. Even his heart, something he'd never relied on before, told him he needed to ensure that Elizabeth was around for the duration. Whatever the hell that might mean to the two of them.

After Elizabeth checked on his wound, he was cleared to go out. After taking a couple of over-the-counter meds, he did feel better. After showing her around the house he would be living in, they sat and had a glass of iced tea before leaving again. He had to admit that Elizabeth was easy to talk to and to have a conversation with. While most people thought conversation and talking were the same, it was as different as night and day.

Talking to someone was just that. The weather was talked about and what they'd done today. Nothing earth-shattering. But having a conversation meant that it was more in debt. More personal. Also, opinions were offered up and talked over as well. He liked that about Elizabeth.

When they got to the first house, he noticed that he was comparing it to his home. So was Elizabeth. The counters in the kitchen weren't as expansive as the ones in his home. The bathroom was smaller than the one on the first floor. They also talked about the yard and what they'd do with it if the house were theirs. Nothing came to mind but to plow it all under and start anew.

"I think we're doing this all wrong," Robert asked her what she meant. Elizabeth smirked. "You and I know that our families are pushing us to be a couple. I love your house, and short of me telling you to get out of it so I can have it, I'm going to move in with you. Purely for selfish reasons."

"Okay." Robert smiled and shook his head. "I'm not at all sure how to respond to that." She laughed. "What will your grandda say when he figures out you're making me a wanton man?"

"He'll be asking us when there will be children so that when he does retire, he'll have someone to go fishing with. Do you fish?" Robert told her that he'd not been in some time, but he did enjoy doing it. "I've never been. I didn't have the opportunity to go, but I never thought of it as something I'd enjoy. However, grandda is talking about going camping and having a long trip to different fishing places. I think I could get a kick out of—you never answered me about me moving in." She charged on when Robert looked at a loss for words. "I hope you're aware I'm only moving into the house, not your bed. I don't think we're at that point in whatever this is between us to jump into bed together. I like you, don't get me wrong, but I'm not sure that it's to the point where we make promises to each other. I love your home, like you, and it suits us both. What do you think?"

Robert chuckled. "You never asked but told me that you were moving in, so I never thought it required an answer. However, I don't have a problem with you moving in. I think I'd like that idea as much as you do. I think it would be great if your great-grandda lived there as well. I like him a great deal, and I know that he would love to be around me when I mess up his company, and he needs to beat the crap out of me." He realized that he did want to have both. She was at his house and the company that her great-grandda had offered him. Living with Elizabeth would never be boring or not without fun.

~*~

Elizabeth loved the fast pace of the emergency room. She didn't want people hurting, but she did enjoy the way she never had the same day twice. When Darrel joined her in the ER, she asked him what was happening.

"I was told there was a house fire on Route Forty, and they asked me to come in and lend a hand if they needed it. Have you had much experience with fire victims?" She told him that Chicago had many fires in the winter months. "I think I might have known that. I don't know much about this fire, but they're working to keep it contained. A residential fire caught a couple of houses on either side. Regarding people being inside when it started, I know a family was in the home, but I haven't heard if they got out. But a firefighter was hurt badly."

Almost as soon as he told her what else he knew about the fire, the first ambulance pulled up. She'd heard the public announcement where she was, but she'd been too busy to focus on what was being said. The little boy she'd been helping with needed fourteen stitches in his arm and leg. He'd been playing around with his dad's two-person saw, and it fell on him, causing so many cuts that she worried about his blood loss.

The two of them worked side by side at times. Elizabeth was also working with most of the ER staff as more and more people were brought in. As she had the most experience with fire victims, she was delegated to be the person who decided if their injuries were a priority or not. It was tough to make that kind of decision, but with everyone coming in, it had to be done that way.

Elizabeth was exhausted when no more people came in from the fire. Going to the nurse's station to nap, she found Robert there talking with Darrel. He'd brought them in some dinner.

"I just realized that I'm starving." She was surprised to see so much food coming out of the bags he'd brought. Not only was there Chinese food, which she loved, but there were subs and several boxed pizzas that he had brought for the rest of the staff. "That's nice of you. Do you make it a habit of doing things like this? It's lovely of you."

"Usually, one of us will help when we can, even if it's only making calls to families in an emergency. I don't know if you noticed or not, being so busy, but my mom is operating the desk out front, and my grandda is holding babies for people that just need a break." She said she'd not noticed much of anything but the person in front of her. "I can understand that. It's been hectic."

She filled her plate with food. The staff came in to get something to eat too. The pizzas and the bottled water cases were going fast, so Darrel called in a second order to be brought in. Elizabeth finally had her fill and figured she'd return to work as soon as she sat there for just a few more minutes. She leaned back and closed her eyes for just a moment.

Waking up, she found herself on one of the few pull-out beds in the nurse's station. She hadn't realized she'd been that exhausted. She stood up and folded the light blanket she'd been covered with. Looking around, she could see that the room had been cleaned up of their mess; all the boxes and bags were also missing. One of the nurses came in when she came out of the bathroom.

"You look much better. My goodness, that man of yours is a godsend. He's out there now helping with the cleanup. They asked me to come in and check on you. My goodness, Doctor Monroe, I have to tell you I'd work for you any day of the week. You're the best doc we've had in the ER department in a long while." She asked her what they'd been putting up with before she'd come in. "Well, I don't like to talk about the other doctors, but since you've done such a good thing for the nurses here, I'll tell you. Doc Wendell, he's on a floater shift now; he berates the nurses in front of the patients and calls them names when his orders are questioned. Just the other day, he wanted one of the staff here to give a dose of morphine to a small one. Enough to knock a bear out, I'm telling you. We have to take it from him because we don't have enough doctors to work in this department. I'm sure he will have a word or two to say to you when you work together. Like he's in charge. Which he's not, by the way. And that his way has worked for the last two years; I kid you not, he thinks that's a long time for a doctor, and he won't put up with anyone overstepping him. Jackass."

"I thank you for the heads up. I've been an ER doctor for eight years, so I've seen my share of men like him." She thought about the gossip that the woman had told her. However, it wasn't the first time she'd heard about Jacob Wendell, so she didn't say anything about it. "Is there anything that I can do to help out? I feel horrible that I took a nap while the rest of you have been working all this time."

"Don't you worry about it. You did us all a favor by being here when we needed you. Besides, we've only been here for a shift. This will be your third shift in a row, and you needed it." Embarrassed by the compliment, she made her way out into the central part of the department. People were still filling up all the chairs, but they didn't look like they'd been fire victims. Finding Robert talking on his cell phone, he kissed her on the mouth as soon as she was close enough to touch.

"Yes, I'm aware of that, Mr. James. However, as I've told you several times, there isn't any way I can do it for you. The staff here has been on duty since the fire began, and I'm not going to leave here to tell you that I'm not going to take your case. As I have told you several times already." Elizabeth sat in the chair that he indicated while he continued to speak to Mr. James. "Yes, sir. I understand this is important, but I will not retake your case. You'll have to find someone else to do it." Robert put it on speaker phone so that she could hear as well.

"I don't give a good god damn about your thinking that you've seen the destruction that went on with this fire and can't defend them because you're a pussy. I want my grandchildren to have the best there is, and short of going there and making you do it, you'd be better off just doing it for me as I have told you to do. Now, I'm not going to be telling you this again, young man; you get your ass over to the police station and do whatever it takes to get them out of there. They're just kids."

Elizabeth put out her hand to have him not speak. She wanted to tell this man off but also to be professional about it, up to a point. There wasn't any way she would be taking his shit right now.

"Mr. James, there are fourteen people that were killed because of the actions of your grandsons. Not only that, but two firefighters are fighting for their lives. One other has died from his injuries." He asked her who she was and whether she knew whom she was talking to. "I'm the doctor at the hospital where the families are trying to deal with their losses. Shut the fuck up; I'm speaking now. I'm sure that you think your grandchildren are above such things as the law. However, they're not. I'm sure they're murdering these people means nothing to them because it doesn't seem to mean shit to you. You're wrong. I'm going to testify that they were responsible for these deaths as much as if they had taken out a gun and killed them. You should get off your high horse, get your ass down here, and talk to the family that lost their four children in the fire because your fucking grandkids decided that it would be fun to see people scrambling out of the house they deliberately set fire to."

"You can't talk to me that way. Listen here, you little bitch. I'm going to own you in about an hour." Robert disconnected the call, pulled her into his arms, and kissed her. Wrapping her arms around his neck, she felt every part of his body pressed against hers, and she wanted more. As soon as he pulled back, she was both hurt and so aroused that she thought she would have to rape the man before it occurred to her that they were in a public setting.

"That went far fast. I'm not saying I didn't enjoy it, but damn woman, you're delicious." She giggled, and he smiled at her. "That's a sound that I could get used to hearing. I know we're rushing things along again here, but I'm falling in love with you, Elizabeth. I'm not sure, but I believe I've been in love with you since I met you. Was it only a couple of weeks ago?"

"Yes. And I believe that I've fallen in love with you too. The things that—well, everything about you tells me that you're nothing more than you are right now. A good, strong man with values that I can get on board with. Not only that, but you're the kindest man I've ever met." He got down on one knee before her. Elizabeth felt her cheeks pink up at the gesture. "What are you doing?"

"Hush. I've been thinking of nothing else since I kissed you. Will you marry me, Elizabeth Monroe? Make me happier every day for the rest of my life. Pamper me. Please make me a father as many times as you wish. Fall deeper in love with me every day?" She told him he was being romantic. "If I weren't, my mother would brain me. I love you, Elizabeth. Will you consent to let me be your husband?"

They'd gathered a large crowd since they'd kissed. The crowd started clapping. Front and center was his grandda. He asked the older man what he thought of having her as his granddaughter. He thought about it for so long that she was sure he would tell her that Robert could do much better than her.

"Well now, I think I like you more than I do him. Not that I don't love the dickens out of him, but I know things about him that his momma doesn't. Having you as a granddaughter would be wonderful. You'll keep him in line, and that'll be good for us all." She asked him if he'd be her grandda as well. "Sure enough, I will be. Even if you didn't marry this one here, I'd be honored to do that for you. But don't you have yourself a grandda?"

"I do. And I love him with all my heart. However,

I think of him more as my father since he raised me as a child. He's a good man, has treated me well over the years, and I couldn't have asked for a better role model. But you, you'll be the grandda to my children and their children, and I think that would be the most wonderful gift I could have from you." He took out his handkerchief and wiped his face. "I didn't mean to upset you."

"You didn't. Not like you think, child. But that's the nicest thing that could have been said to me today." She hugged him then, thinking he was the Archer family's heart. "My missus, she would have been so happy to have you as her granddaughter. And with the others coming along, I think that she'd be tickled pink."

"Well, so am I, Grandda." The two hugged, and it wasn't until Robert cleared his throat rather loudly that she remembered that he'd proposed to her. Laughing, she told him yes and that she'd loved him forever. "I want to have children too — a houseful of them. I don't care whether they're of our body or someone else. I want to give every child the same chance I had."

Someone from the crowd hollered out for him to kiss her. Elizabeth giggled.

"I love you." When Robert stood up, she kissed him again. It was no less heated, but it was quicker than before. The crowd began to cheer for them, and it wasn't until she heard the emergency sound go off that she realized she needed to get home. She'd been here long enough. Telling that to Robert, he agreed with her. "We have plenty to do tonight in that we need to set up some furniture for us, so I like that idea."

There was some furniture in the house they would be living in but not enough for them to entertain and for themselves. It had all been taken out and stored when the renovations began. While she knew this, she wondered if there would be room for the things she still had at her place in Chicago. Elizabeth asked Robert about it on their way to the house.

"I've been in the house, of course, but not enough to know about bedrooms. Peter assured me that we could raise a large family in it if we wanted. They had a few of the bedrooms enlarged too. Also, there is a nursery and a ballroom on the upper floors. He and Heather had decided to make that the main suite, and I thought it was also a good idea." She agreed with him. When they pulled up in front of the house, there weren't as many trucks as when they'd been here a couple of days ago. "I wonder if they're about finished up. I mean, it's only just after two. I'd think they'd still be working."

"Since you own the company now, do you think they're testing you to see if they can slack off?" He said that he hoped not. "Yeah, me either. Grandda would have a cow."

When they walked up to the house, she noticed a couple of the larger pieces of the large equipment were missing. Also, a large trailer in the back had been used to haul the more significant amounts. On it was a smaller earth mover and several tall stacks of outdoor brick. She asked Robert about it.

"I'm not sure, to be honest. However, I'd feel better if you'd call your grandda to come here. While I don't know what might be happening, if it's all good, we can talk to him about staying with us. What do you think?" She agreed. "Before I forget, your grandda is going to sell the old house that the two of you lived in. He said that he wants a place to make his memories in. not one that will be fighting for memories of the past with your grandmother."

Calling her grandda, she told him that things were slacking at the construction site, and he said he was on his way. Elizabeth hadn't even been aware that it had been announced that Robert would be taking over. Grandda told her he'd not said a word, but they might have figured it out with things going on. He told her he'd be bringing the police with him, just in case of trouble.

She had no idea, but she thought that was an excellent way to handle this. As soon as she was in the doorway, she could hear shouting. Then the calm voice of Robert. She thought he was taking it fairly well, whatever was going on, until she entered the kitchen.

"You're going to put that gun away, Mr. Conley, or I'll have Elizabeth here call the police. Whatever you've stolen from here—" Mr. Conley, a man who had been with the company for years, said he wasn't stealing shit that was owed to him. "While I've told you I'm taking over the company, I don't have all the rules figured out yet. So if you'd explain to me why the stuff you've taken and the things you've yet to take are owed to you, I'd be greatly appreciative."

"I told you. I'm taking this stuff because of that woman. Archer was her name." It bothered her that he'd said 'was' her name. "She came in this morning telling us we'll have to hire more men to work here so the house will be finished sooner. We're working hard as we can. I told her she needed to get her fanny home, and she got angry with me and fired us all. And she told me that we wouldn't be paid anymore either."

"Since I have two sisters-in-law and my mom, I'm not sure which Archer you're speaking about," Conley told Robert that it was Heather. "Okay. I know her. But I feel it was more than just her telling you that she wanted the house finished sooner. What else did the two of you argue about? I know she can be a light on the intense side, but she'd never fire anyone in my company without having a good reason to do that."

Heather walked into the room. "I told him that he was fired because when I got here this morning, after keeping an eye on them last night, I noticed that he was taking things off the lot we paid for. Not only that, but I've been to the store, and it seems he's purchased several room air conditions, four microwaves, and several thousand dollars worth of plants and trees that we didn't discuss beforehand." Elizabeth could see that Heather was spitting mad and loved it. "Not only did I fire him, but I also sent the police out to his home last night, and they watched him and his son planting the trees in their yard that didn't belong to him. In addition, the fucker took the backhoe to his home with your company and several other things that I have no name for that had, until this morning, Monroe Construction on them. Now they're painting Conley Construction on all the pieces."

"I've called in the police." Conley eyed the door when Grandda Archer said that. "You try anything stupid, well, stupider right now, and I'm going to have to shoot you in the knee, Conley. You know I carry, and it would be a shame to get blood in this house too."

Chapter 2

Mary was depressed. Not only was she so depressed that she didn't want to go on with this sham of a life, but she was also pissed off that the only thing that Katie had gotten was a broken leg—it couldn't have been her neck, oh no. It pissed her off the most that she was free to move around, and all Mary could do was sit on her cot in a jail cell.

"Ms. Pencil, are you listening to me?" She waved the judge off. She didn't feel like dealing with him today. "I'm not going to be able to work with you today if you're not even going to pay attention."

"What do you care? How does anyone care how I feel about any of the shit going on?" Before he could bang his gavel, telling her to watch her language, she continued. "Do you know how difficult it was to kill off our parents so that we could live the life we deserved? No one knows the suffering we had to endure to have things our way. Even after all the planning, mother had to go on living for a little while afterward. She was going to tell on us; she told James and me. You've no idea how much we enjoyed letting her know that her little plans to send us to boarding school weren't going to work now. She thought that separating us would be the best thing for us. That we would be able to make friends. Friends? James and I were all we needed in the world, but she and father wouldn't have it. See what that did for them? Then, after they were gone, someone came to the house and took us to Katie. Oh my god, you have no idea how hard that was on us. Even after trying to kill her off, she survived. Mother always said that about her, that her sister was a survivor. So James and I settled in for the long run. Even after she married and Del always took up her time, James tried to poison them. Nothing worked even after the kids started to pop out. Christ. Even killing them off one by one became a nightmare."

"You tried to kill your aunt and uncle and their children? For what reason?" She told the judge that they wanted to be by themselves. "It's against the law for minors to be left to their own devices. However, in your and your brother's case, there might not have been so many deaths associated with your names. Weren't they good to you? They didn't treat you well?"

"Of course, they treated us all right. But that's not the point, now is it? That's not what we wanted. Mother often called us deviants. She even put locks on our doors so we'd not be together." She could see on his face that he'd figured it out without her saying the words. "What difference did it make to anyone that we were in love? That we were all we needed. But again and again, people got into our way of happiness. It's their fault that they're dead. They had no right to get into our business."

"You murdered them for trying to do the right thing." She stood up as best she could and shouted at him, wondering who was in charge of saying what was right or wrong. "The law. The very reason that you're here today. Also, the reason that your brother is dead."

"My brother is dead because Katie Archer thought having her children would be all right with us. Had she asked and done what we wanted, none of this would have been necessary. She thought that having children of her own would make us happy. It didn't. She forever cared for them when we deserved to be the only ones she waited on when we wanted something. Katie never pampered us as we deserved, either. She never cooked us all the things that we wanted. Then when we left her home, thank god, she came to see us as if we'd be happy to see her. Why did we move across the world to get away from her and her brats if they would show up when they wanted? We had to set her right on that too."

"Did Katie make you watch her children? Did she make you care for them in any way? Take on more chores around the house? What did she do to you that had you wanting to harm her and the children?" Mary told the judge they were never asked to do anything for the kids. But that they did have to clean up their rooms. "So, for very little payback on your part, you set out to murder Del and Katie Archer and their six children. For no reason that I can see other than you were spoilt."

"So? It's not like we didn't deserve to be treated differently. James and I were special, and they should have seen that. Even before she came around, we were going places. Then she had to fuck that all up by not only treating us like everyone else, but she even got into our business when we explicitly told her to stay away from us." He asked her if she was referring to her children being given up. "Of course. Christ. If she had kept her nose out of what we were doing, James would still be alive, and we'd be making our way into life as it should have been all along."

"Giving up your children for adoption, you mean." She rolled her eyes at him and told him not to be so stupid. "I'm trying very hard to understand all this, Ms. Pencil. You blame a woman who gave up her single life to raise you and your brother. Not at a small cost, either. Not only did she raise you, but she seemed to have ensured you were safe. I'm trying my best to figure out why you're able to sit there and blame your aunt for your lot in life. Some of the things on this list of crimes you've committed with your brother were things that I was positive you did without any cause from Katie. Like the death of your cook. Several people here are presumed dead that you and James admitted to killing before you were even in Katie's life. How is that even remotely possible that you think to blame her?"

"You don't understand how special we were. No one does, and that's what gets them dead. Katie messed up our lives, and I have every right to blame her for everything that has gone wrong—even the death of my wonderful brother." Mary stared at the judge as he looked at her. "Well? Are you going to let me go, or do I have to make arrangements to have your head blown off? I'm not above asking Katie for the money to do it. She owes me so much as it is now that she'll pay or be dead herself."

You just threatened a judge, Ms. Pencil. Haven't you learned anything from being in the courtroom about doing such a thing?" She told him to fuck off; she knew that she was in the right. "In this, and many other things, you are not only not correct, but you couldn't be more wrong. I'm going to sentence you now. It's my great pleasure to condemn you to seventy-four life terms in federal prison with no chance of parole. I could add more, but I won't. Unless you think you're too special not to be given everything you have coming to you? I believe that several lifetimes behind bars will keep you off the streets and out of the Archer family's lives, and the world will be a safer place all the way around."

"What the hell is wrong with you? Did you not just hear me tell you to get me out of jail? I'm not going to go back to that place." He told her that she wasn't. "Well, good. You're finally getting your head out of your ass. When can I get this shit off me and back where I belong? I'm sick of this shit not going my way."

"You're to be remanded to federal prison as soon as you can be taken away. I'm going to make sure that you're well cared for on the way. It would be best if you didn't die before you have time to enjoy your new life. I know that I will." The man beside him leaned in to whisper to him, and the judge smiled at her. Finally, she thought, he was getting on board with her demands. "I have a note here from your lovely Aunt Katie. Let me read it to you."

"Dearest Niece, Mary Pencil. I will not be coming to visit you while you are incarcerated. None of the family will. Your ex-husband is raising your child and is much happier than you imagine. James' children are also excited, living a life they should have had from their father. Comfortable and without any threats to their wellbeing. Nor will you be given any numbers or phone time to call me asking for things. As of this moment, I wash my hands of you. I have arranged, just for you, that you will have to work for anything extra that you'll need while serving your time — no special treatment. There will be no treats for your birthday or holidays.

"James has been cremated, and his ashes will stay at the funeral home until you're dead. Then the two of you will be buried in the same nameless prison plot with only your number as reference to who you were."

The judge looked at her when she told him that she wanted Katie there so she could have a few words with her. Then she asked him for a weapon so that she could make her see reason.

"That isn't going to happen; I'm happy to say. She and her family are enjoying a lovely day, celebrating that you and James are no longer a problem. Now, let me finish this. Now, where was I? Oh yes. There we are."

"Mary, when I think of what you and your brother said, I should have taken action against the two of you then. I might well have been able to save a few more people." The judge looked at her again before reading on. *"You have the life you deserve, and I will also. Your Aunt Katherine Archer."*

Before she could think about what Katie had said to her, she was shoved out the door and into an awaiting van. No amount of threats, which usually worked for her, would make the people in the van with her stop so that she could get out. Someone was going to pay for this, and she would keep at them until they finally gave in. That had worked for her before all this shit began to fall on her. The van stopped so suddenly that she nearly fell off her seat. Mary might have if not for the fact that she was chained up.

"What the fuck was that for? You morons are

going to pay for this." The back of the van opened, and
she looked at the man standing there. She didn't know
what he thought he might be doing, but she knew a sap
when she saw one. "Paul, I have no idea what you think
will happen when I get out of here, but you'd better be
straightening up your act. And I do hope that you got rid
of that brat. I will not be aged by — "

The cop across from her fell over. If he was dead, it
was good. It would be one less person that she'd have to
kill to get out of her. The second cop fell over too. But he
winked at her first. Not knowing what was going on, she
watched him as he lay there. As soon as he was down on
the floor, she felt the locks on her legs let go. It only took
her two seconds to get the chain unwrapped from her
seat, and she was on the move.

Peter picked up the gun lying on the floor next to
the second cop. Not sure when it had been pulled free,
she reached for it at the same time that Paul pointed it at
her.

"What the fuck do you think you're doing? Put
that shit away. Or better yet, hand it to me. You deserve
to die as much as the next person. Hand it over, Paul, or
help me; I'll make you suffer in ways you can imagine."
Paul told her that he hated her. "Well, la-dee-da. I've

hated you since we first met. Give me the fucking—"

The pain in her chest hurt. While she didn't bother looking at what had happened, she knew enough that she was shot. Turning to look at the cop behind her, the second shot hit her face. Mary was hurting by the time she fell to her knees.

"I only had to distract you enough so they could shoot you in the back, Mary. They swear that they'd been knocked out when the van suddenly stopped for a deer that ran out in front of them. I thought that was a fitting ending for you. To be less important than a wild animal. Having you dead will lessen my son's nightmares of you and make everyone, in general, feel better at night." She began to think she was hurt worse than she thought she might have been. "You'll be thrilled—or perhaps not, I could care less that I've met someone that makes me happy. And when we marry, I'm going to be thrilled beyond words. So lucky that you'll never be a thought in my head until the day that I die. Fuck you, Mary Pencil. I hope you rot in hell."

~*~

Robert saw the cruiser pull into the driveway where he was working at his home that he and Elizabeth would be moving into full-time soon. Just yesterday, Markus

Conley was arrested, as had been his wife and son. The things that they'd been stealing from construction sites were vast. Not only had they been stealing from the job they'd caught him on, but his theft had been going on since the first-week Bingo hired him. He'd not even tried to hide the money that was in his bank account and safety deposit box. Conley bragged about them thinking; Robert supposed that no one could get into them without his permission. Idiot.

"Robert." He asked Officer Carter if he was all right as he tipped his imaginary hat in return for the gesture. "I am. Thank you so much for asking. I came to let you know that Mary is dead. She was trying to escape when the van she was riding in was in a near miss with a deer. When they slammed on their brakes, both the officers were hurt, and she took their key to get out—the damnest thing about that. However, I hit one of them suckers once. Not a thing that I'd like to have repeated. The two men in the back were knocked unconscious, and she took their keys. After getting herself unlocked from the van, one of the men woke in time to shoot her. Good thing if you ask me. The government doesn't need to pay for her to sit around on her fat ass for—I'm sorry, Robert. I forgot that she was related to you for a moment."

"That's all right, Ryan. I'm with you on this being a good thing." He nodded and looked around the house they were both standing in. The need to change the subject seemed like a good idea. "It's coming along well, I think. After the insurance company reimburses us for all the stolen equipment, we'll be working well. Merce and Del replaced what was needed now so we could finish up, and the insurance company was good with that."

The two of them talked about the renovations that were going on. Mostly they admired the stained glassed pieces that would go into the house as soon as the window areas were enlarged or cut down, depending on what was going on in the room. The staircase was one of the places where a more significant part was going. Just at the top of the stairs, they were going to put a couple of chairs and a small table to read by. Robert thought the light through the glasswork would be distracting, but he wanted what Elizabeth wanted. Ryan asked him if he knew if Peter was going to sell off the other pieces are not.

"I know Peter and Heather will let the family go through it all to take what we want. I've taken a couple of the larger pieces to put in the window openings. I couldn't believe how many of those we've found stored in the barn and basement of the house." Ryan told him how he remembered his grandmother. "I don't have many memories of her. I remember more when I see a picture of her with the family. I know that grandda misses her something terrible."

Ryan was an older man, more than likely older than his grandfather. While he was on the police force, had been since he'd been just a kid, he told him, Ryan didn't do much other than run errands for the department and make out the schedule when there were events that the police were needed for nowadays. His wife had passed away some time ago, and he was lonely; he told him, so working kept him out of trouble.

"Your grannie, she sure could make a person feel good about themselves. You don't know my daddy; he was a bastard and a half. Mostly it was drinking that made him so mean. Your grannie would take my brothers, sisters, and me into her house and keep us there until our daddy was out of jail or off his drinking after momma died. Daddy died about the time I was out of college. The rest of us scattered to the four winds and never looked back. I miss them." Robert told him he didn't know what to do without his family nearby. "You had a good set of parents, Robert. They loved you and supported you no matter what you did. Though we never had a lick of trouble with you when you boys were younger."

"Mom and dad would have murdered us if we caused any trouble that we couldn't explain." Ryan laughed and asked if he was talking about the middle school girl. "Yes. Bethany James. Her parents were ill, pneumonia if I remember correctly. I went there after school to give her the homework she was missing. I found her not only exhausted but also caring for her parents and little sister. I put her to bed and stayed to help her out all night. I forgot to tell my parent where I was; I'd worried about them. We didn't have cell phones as we do now. When mom and dad showed up there, mom was ready to beat me for staying all night with a young girl when she found James' not just in need of more help than a couple of teenagers could give them but that her little sister was ill as well."

"Your parents, after calling in an ambulance to get the help they needed, took that baby home to care for. I think your daddy gave little Anna away when she got married." Robert remembered only then that Mr. James had passed away from his illness, and his wife had been ill for the rest of her life. Robert smiled at the memory of dad being so flustered when he'd been asked. "As I said, you have good parents. Even your grandparents were good people."

"Thanks, Ryan. I know that, but it is nice to hear someone else say it too." He hugged him before he left, telling Robert that he only had to ask if he needed anything from him. "I will. Thank you for coming over and telling me about Mary."

Robert called his mom to let her know about her niece. He had a feeling that even though Mom had said she was washing her hands of the woman, she would still grieve for her. It did help her that Del and Merce had adopted James' three children. And that Paul had moved to the area so that Mom and the others could be a part of his son Brian's life. The kids spent a great deal of time together at Mom's house, and he thought they were making the best memories with her and Grandda.

The crew that he was working with was a good bunch. Bingo, his future grandfather-in-law, was around enough that Robert never felt like he was messing up too much. He was forming a good bond with the older man as well. Elizabeth was working for the rest of the morning into the afternoon, so he was here making sure he didn't get into trouble being left alone. Smiling, he thought of how exhausted Elizabeth had been when they'd gotten home last night.

She'd kept dozing while he was driving her back from her work. Every once in a while, she'd wake up enough to tell him something, but for the most part, she slept. Even when they pulled up in front of the house, she was too tired to walk inside on her own, and he ended up carrying her up to the bedroom he'd been sleeping in. Robert took the couch in the living room so as not to disturb her excessively.

"Mr. Robert?" He had to get used to his new name now, he thought, wondering how many times Bash — he didn't know if it was his last or first name — had called to him. "Mr. Robert, there is something that you gotta see. It's amazing that we even saw it before tearing out the wall completely."

Following the man, Robert wasn't upset about the interruption as he was relieved by it. His thoughts about Elizabeth waking him up with a very carnal kiss made him want to go to the hospital and tear her clothes off. The kitchen resembled a wartime room. It had been ravaged by all the walls being taken out. Bingo and his grandda were in the room too.

The door was beautiful. Asking if either of them knew why the oak door had been closed off, neither of them knew. Not only had the door been plastered over to hide the fact that it was in the kitchen, but it had also been written on. Getting closer to the fancy script, he was surprised to read what was there. The date on it was eighteen fifty-one.

"This here room was for my mamma. She passed on before I could get it all done for her." There were many misspelled words, but he could make them out. *"She wasn't a good mamma, but I made me a promise with my daddy, and I was beholding to do it for her. But she's dead now. So whoever found this, you can have her things for your own if'n you want them. Otherwise, lit you a big old fire and have at it."*

The key to the door was hanging on the frame, and Robert used it to unlock the door. The darkness of the room and cobwebs hanging in the opening made it difficult to see anything inside. Taking one of the pieces of wood just lying around, he removed all the dusty cobwebs and went inside.

"There doesn't seem to be any electricity in this room. Let me get one of those big lights to put on the situation." As soon as Bingo returned with the light, he walked into the darkened cavern and had his first look at what had been stored away. "My goodness, Robert, this is wonderful."

It was too. It was a beautiful turn-of-the-century bedroom set, consisting of not just the dressers and bed but a sizeable tall boy, bedside tables, a large blanket chest, and a woman's vanity table. He ran his finger over the top of the dresser and saw that the wood looked dark.

"If I don't miss my bet on that, I'd say that's mahogany. I've not seen a set like that in forever. My goodness. I'm betting that would make a good guest set if you'd like to have it cleaned up." He said he would, but he'd have to see what Elizabeth thought of it. "Yes, sir. That's a good thought. I'm positive she'll love it as much as you seem to."

"I do love it. I think that it would look amazing in the room down the hall. The one at the end." Bingo asked if it was the one with the big picture window facing the backyard. "Yes, that's the one. The dark wood with the sun shining on it would be breathtaking. Look, there is even clothing in the cabinet here."

He was about as excited as he could be about the find. The more they looked around, the more that they uncovered. Robert loved the ladies grooming set that was on the vanity. Beautiful bottles of now empty perfume bottles. Even though there wasn't a bathroom in the large room, handmade soaps and loofas were still in their skin.

"I'm betting your mom would love some of those seeds in that thing. She's been talking about starting them up since I moved in with her. Those are old seeds too. And from their size, I'd say they never came out of a package, either. Just heirloom seeds passed around the town until most of them forgot to save them. You take that thing over to your mom, and she'll grow them for fifty years or so." He did like that idea as well. While he'd never used a loofa, he had heard great things about them.

Robert's excitement grew as they found a window that had been boarded over. Once the boards were removed, the room looked larger. Bingo asked him what he was going to do with the extra space.

"I've not thought beyond how many things are in this room. But I think that it would make a great pantry. Or even a breakfast area. Whatever Elizabeth wants." He decided to message her to see if she was busy. When she called him back, he'd already figured out how to show her the room. After telling her the story that had come with it, she also wanted to see the furniture. "Grandda thinks that it's mahogany. I know that it's heavy. You would have laughed at us all while we were trying to move a couple of pieces to get to the window."

"I love it. And it has a rich history behind it. Yes, the bedroom you were talking about would show it off in the best light. Oh, how I wish I were there. But we've gotten a lot done today since we weren't all that busy. Also, Merce was here putting in a couple of pieces of equipment. I had no idea she owns the company that makes most of the things we use here."

"That's why I think she and Del are perfectly matched. Not only are the two of them engineers, but they seem to see things outside of the box more than anyone else I know." After telling her that he'd be here waiting for her to get off at three, he said to her that he loved her. "With all that I am, my dear Elizabeth."

"You're such a sap. But I do you as well." She was still laughing when he put his cell phone back in his pocket. The others had left when he began talking to Elizabeth, so he had the entire room to himself. Pulling out one of the drawers to look at whatever had been left behind, he found a book of sorts.

"I came by—what do you have there, son?" He handed the book over to his mother, and she flipped through a few of the pictures before shivering. "It's a death book. During the Victorian times, though I never heard much of it being done here, someone used to take pictures of the dead in posing pictures with family members so that they could be remembered. If I remember correctly, it was called Memento Mori photography, which means remember you must die. I think it was mostly children that died when they were so young. They thought it would lessen the pain of a loved one's death if they could see them all together. My goodness, those are the best I've seen, considering what they happen to be."

"I think that the family that lived here, or the man's in-laws took them for people. This is his portfolio, I suppose." Mom shivered again and handed the book to him. "I'm sure you didn't come out here to see what I'd found, did you?"

"In a way, yes. Delmar told me about the room you'd unearthed, and I thought it would be fun to see what is in here. The furniture is beautiful." The two went through the doors and the cabinet to see what else they could find. "You should donate these dresses to someone that can put them on display. I'm not sure who that would be, but it would make an excellent addition to someone that collects things like this. She must have been a big woman, this mother-in-law of his. These dresses are huge."

They both laughed but did sober up when they

thought of what they were doing. Mom told him she was slightly nervous about the book and trying to make a joke. She apologized to him.

"No need for that, mom. I know it made me feel a little off when I found it. The one with the baby and the little girl got me shaken up, the worse. I can't imagine doing something like that for a living." Mom told him that she couldn't either. "Let's look at the bedroom where this set will go in. I already spoke to Elizabeth. She also loves the idea of putting it in the one at the end of the hall."

When Elizabeth showed up, the room was measured to see where the pieces would go. The house has eleven bedrooms in it. After it was finished on the second floor, there would only be five. Dividing the rooms up, they were larger seemed to be just what needed to be done. Also, more plumbing. Not just for the second floor but the upper level as well. Elizabeth didn't want to look at the book they'd found. She said she'd had a shitty day and couldn't take any more death right now.

"Come here and let me hold you." She went to him willingly, and when his mom walked out of the room, he lifted her chin to see that she was crying. Kissing her cheeks where the tears had fallen, he told her again that he loved her. "I will forever love you. You know that, don't you, Elizabeth? I wish I could take away your pain right now."

"It's all right. I'm all right now. I hate to see children die. The little boy that came into the department had been ill for a long time. I think that his parents knew this was the last time for him, but it was still difficult for them to let him go." She cried a little more. Robert held her tightly in his arms. "Let's take your mom to dinner, then go home and have crazy wild sex all over the place."

"You've got a deal." Mom didn't want to go with them; she had jam ready to be sealed up. The two didn't want to drive much to eat, so they settled on a pizza and sodas for dinner and ate it in their kitchen. Nothing much was in there yet, but they did talk about the extra room they now had.

Chapter 3

Elizabeth loved that they could be so happy together, standing in the kitchen at a makeshift counter having a pizza. The pop was all right, but since the refrigerator hadn't arrived yet, they didn't have any ice-cold water. Robert told her he'd not had a pop in about ten years.

"I don't think I've missed anything by not drinking it. When mom decided she didn't care for sweet tea anymore and cut out the caffeine, we all did the same. Not for solidarity but because since she didn't make it for us when we came over, we didn't either." Robert laughed, and she had to smile. "The first time I had tea at a nice restaurant, it was so bad that I thought I would be sick. Since I felt I needed something to drink with dinner, I ended up with water. The restaurant charged me seven bucks for a glass of water that I'm sure they got out of the taps in the kitchen."

Making their way up to the bedroom that Elizabeth had been using since moving in with him, the two talked again about the furniture for the other room and their plans for their own space. He wanted it to be whatever she wanted. However, she told him that he was to have an opinion or he might well end up sleeping on the sofa in the living room again. Laughing, he asked her please don't do that to him.

"I would love a bedroom set that has a history. Not bad things; however, I'm not sure we could find anything old that didn't have some nasty business. Also, I'd like to have plenty of room in the bedroom. We can walk around with lots of space without falling over each other." She said she liked that as well. "A large bathroom too. One with a tub and shower, not in the same place. Two commodes on either side of it so that we could have a little privacy. I want hardwood floors in here. I know that floors can be cold when we get up, but the feeling of the nice warm wood would be a comfort to me too."

"I love all those ideas. We can make that happen

because it's still early in the renovations." While she didn't know how to make it happen, Elizabeth was sure that her grandda would help him to make his granddaughter as happy as Robert wanted her. "I want to make love to you. All night long."

"I'd like that as well." She moved toward him, telling him everything she wanted to do to his body. "Touching you is a priority to me. Feeling your flesh beneath my fingers. Massaging your muscles until they're soft."

Pulling her to him, he kissed her as he unbuttoned her blouse. Pulling it off her and dropping it to the floor, he pulled back enough to see that she wasn't wearing a bra. She wanted him to see her as a woman in love. More than that, she wanted him to love her forever and a day because she loved him that much.

"I want to see you. All of you." He asked her if she was going to take his clothing off. "No. If I started on that, I'd never get to finish. I'd be too distracted by what I uncover."

"Thank you." He unbuttoned his shirt and tossed it over his shoulder. "Why don't you take off your things too? I'd like to see if the real you even come close to what I have been thinking about for so long."

She obliged him by stripping off her pants and panties simultaneously. Since she'd removed her shoes earlier, she was naked for him. Robert seemed to be distracted for a moment. He was staring at her like she was something that he'd feast on. There wasn't a place on her body that she didn't want him to explore and taste. When she reminded him, none too gently, by poking him in the ribs that he wasn't naked with her, he nearly killed himself, tearing his pants off before taking off his belt. Elizabeth laughed at him when he had to take several breaths to calm himself before trying again.

When she stepped toward him, wrapping her hand around his cock, she knew he was as close to coming as she was. Dropping to her knees before him, she took him into her mouth and swallowed his thick head beyond the tightness of her throat. Christ, she would come soon if she didn't pace herself.

"Christ, Elizabeth. I'm coming." His cock filled her mouth repeatedly as he fucked her this way. Feeling his cum splash down her throat had her coming as well. Crying out with his cock still inside her mouth, she held onto his legs so that she'd not miss anything of him if she fell back on her butt.

Robert pulled from her mouth, picked her up

from the floor, and put her on the bed. He was between her thighs and eating her pussy as she tried to get her bearings. She came three times hard enough to make her eyes roll to the back of her head. Even begging him to stop so that she could catch her breath hadn't stopped him from making her come again.

She could only marvel at his size and girth when he stood up between her legs. His cock was full again, the crown of him dark with need. Reaching out to touch him, take the little bit of precum that was there for her to taste, he moved back.

"You touch me now, and I won't be able to be inside you when I come. I need to fill you, love." She nodded and moved further on the bed as he asked her to do. "You looked like every dream I've had of you since I met you. You're so beautiful."

"Fuck me, Robert." He nearly pounced on her when she commanded him to take her. As soon as he was over her, his cock at her entrance, she pulled him down to her mouth for a kiss. The moment he entered her, hard and fast, she came three times before he moved. If they made love like this all the time, she'd be nothing but dust by the end of the week.

Robert nibbled at her breasts. He suckled at her

nipples. Just as she was ready to come again, he'd moved over her body in a way that made her see stars and rainbows. He massaged her muscles, making her want to come again. A simple finger at her throat had her breath catch, and her body wanted more.

"I need to come. Please, Robert. Give me what I need." He moved. That was all; he just rolled his hips in a way that had her screaming out his name. The climax — a tame word for such a glorious earth-shattering moment — ripped through her soul and made it Roberts.

She hadn't realized that she had fainted until she opened her eyes. The room was dark, so it told her that it was, hopefully, the same night. Getting up to go to the bathroom, she realized she was alone in the big bed. Reaching for her cell phone to call Robert to ask where he was, she was startled to hear it ringing. Picking it up when Robert's face showed her it was him, Elizabeth smiled. It soon fell when he started talking to her.

"Your grandda has had a stroke and was in a car accident. I'm with him in the hospital now. When he was first found, they didn't know who he was until my brother went to see his injuries. He had the heart attack while driving back to our place for the evening." She asked him if he was all right. "I'm not sure how to answer that. He seems fine. A few cuts and bruises are being stitched up. Before you ask why I didn't tell you what happened, I had to identify him. I wouldn't have mentioned it if it hadn't been your grandda."

"I'm on my way," Robert told her to wait as Del was going there to get her. "I can drive, Robert. I need to see my grandda."

"It was your car that he totaled. You don't have a car there right now." She told him she was sorry. "No need to be. It's a very stressful situation. He's in surgery right now to clean up some wounds on his head. Also, he has a broken arm and sprained ankle. They're keeping an eye on his heart, as you can imagine, so he doesn't have another one. As you can imagine, being around him all your life, he's making a fuss because everyone else is."

"Yes, I can see him doing that. He'd be more upset about that than him being injured." She thought for a moment. "Robert, is he all right? I mean, he's not gone, is he? I don't think I could handle finding out that he's not well and already gone."

"I would never lie to you about that, honey. I promise you he's doing well, considering. He was awake when I was called in, telling me how sorry he was for wrecking your car." Wiping at the tears, she told Robert that she loved him. "And I love you too. When you get here, I'll be on the second floor in the surgery department. Del said he'd pick up something for me to eat when he arrived. Make sure you get something as well. All right?"

"Yes. I will. I'll be there as soon as I can. And if Del doesn't get the lead out of his ass and make sure we get there in a reasonable time, I'm going to murder him." He laughed, which made her feel so much better. "I'm hopping in the shower now and then dressing. I'll be on my way as soon as Del gets here." Going down after her quick shower, the doorbell rang. Opening it up with her shoes in her hand and her bag over her shoulder, she was good to go.

The hospital wasn't that busy, but there were a lot of police around. She didn't know what had them all there but ignored them in favor of going up to the surgery floor. Robert met her at the elevator as she and Del, along with Merce, got off on the same floor. As soon as she was in Roberts's arms, she felt so much better. It was going to be a long wait, but with him there, she thought it wouldn't be so bad.

After two more hours, the doctor came to talk to them. He was smiling, which made her feel so much better. Asking her if she minded if the others heard what he had to say, he began by telling her what everyone seemed to know already. Grandda was a pistol.

"He's doing very well, considering his age. However, I will point out that your grandda is in much better shape than men half his age. I don't think you have to worry about him having any long-term issues with the stroke that they think he had." Robert asked if he thought that he'd not had a stroke. "We took him to surgery to get his noggin taken care of and will need to run more tests to make that a certainty. I believe that he fell asleep at the wheel and nothing more. However, as I said, he will need to have more tests. A better diet too. I understand that he had some dessert after every meal. Even a snack. He should be cutting back on his sugar. At least cut him down to one dessert a day and not all of them. That might make him mad, but he's not getting any younger."

"I've tried that with him before. All it did was make him go elsewhere for his dessert. I'll make it work this time. I'll have to think of something he wants and see if that works." Robert laughed and said that a baby might help. "Yes, there is that. Do you know someone that is giving one away?"

They all laughed, and she felt a great deal of weight

be lifted off her shoulders. Her grandda was all right, and that was all that mattered to her now. As they waited at the hospital for her to be able to see him, the rest of the Archers showed up. Katie brought them some water and things like carrot sticks and celery. She didn't much care for celery but figured that if she was going to make her grandda start eating better, she needed to as well. But after taking one bite of the nasty stringy stuff, she spat it out and ate the carrots. No amount of dressing was going to make that shit taste any better, and she decided that she'd never make her kids or anyone else eat that stuff if they didn't want to.

~*~

Bingo wasn't sure what all the fuss was about, but he undoubtedly was enjoying it. The nurses treated him like a king, and his granddaughter was there every day when she wasn't working. Even then, she'd come up to see him. However, he thought she needed to get on with her own life and not hang around an older man to whom she just happened to be related. Smiling at her when she came into his room, he thought her the prettiest doctor around town. As soon as she sat down, he took her hand into his.

"You need to stop coming here all the time. Didn't

they tell you I was just fine and dandy? I'm not going to get any better with you being here all the time and me worrying about how you're treating that young man of yours." She told him that Robert was doing just fine without her. "I doubt that. He'd do or say just about anything to make you smile, and if you wanted to be here with me, no matter what he wanted, he made sure you were here. Never seen a man so excited to make a woman smile like he is with you."

"He loves me, and I love him." He told her that was as plain as the nose on her face. "Perhaps you should stop telling me to go away and get better so I can have peace with you at home. I miss you hanging out with me when I'm not working."

"I don't miss you. Do you want to know why? Because you're here all the time. Don't you have a life, child? Something other than me to hang around with? I know you do. That poor Robert looks lost without you there with him." She rolled her eyes at him. "Don't be giving me that look, young lady. You know that I'm telling you the truth. Go on home and make a big dinner for—no, that won't work. You can't cook worth crap. Order some of that Chinese food that the two of you like so much and hang out on the couch for the rest of the night. I can't think of another thing that would make me happier than to figure out you two weren't pining away for me to come there."

"You scared me, old man." He said that he scared himself a bit. "I don't know what I would have done if you'd been hurt badly. You have to stick around for me."

"Honey, I don't know if you've figured this out or not, but I'm not going to be living forever. I'm an old man. While I'm in good health, like they told you, I'm wearing down to the nubbin. It's getting harder and harder for me to think about working with them younger men anymore." She told him not to talk like that. "It's a fact of life, Elizabeth. Old people, sometimes younger ones too, die. I'm on the other side of eighty as it is now. Won't be long; come February, I'll be hitting ninety years old. That's a long time for someone hanging around young people."

"You can't leave me." He only looked at her. "All right. I know you will, but I will be a mess when it happens. You know that, don't you? I can't imagine a life where you're not in it. A time when I won't be looking for you to help me with something. Grandda, you're all the family that I have left."

"Now that's not true, and you know it. You have

all the Archers there for you. And anyone else in town that has the sense to get out of the rain can see that you're a good person. Your grannie, she sure did love you to pieces. I want to go and see her again." She looked up at him with tears in her eyes. "Now, don't you be crying about me leaving. It's not going to happen today; I don't think. I want you to be the happiest you can be. Even after I'm gone."

"You make it sound like I'm going to roll you over the hill and forget about you. That's not going to happen, so you know. I'll think of you daily for the rest of my life." He told her that wasn't a bad way to have him sent off. She smacked him on the shoulder. "Don't be that way. I'm not going to waste my energy pushing you over the hill. I'm just going to plant you in the backyard so I can go and tell you how much I don't miss you all the time."

"You be happy like you are right now, and I can die a pleased man. I might even come around sometime and see how you're doing." She said she'd like that. "I would too. However, you could have me a grandbaby before I up and die. That would be a good way for me to think about you too. A little girl just like you. Or even a boy that is the spitting image of Robert. He is a good man, that one."

"He's the best. All of the Archer men are. I hope I can raise my child as Katie did hers." He told her that she'd do a fine job. "I hope so. I'd hate to raise a brat and have you come back to give me hell for it." She stared at him for a moment before speaking. "What is your real name? I know that you weren't named Bingo. I could never get grannie to tell me when she was alive. If I'm going to name my child after you, I should hope I have the correct grandda."

"I'm only willing to tell you this because I know you'd name that baby of yours Bingo just for spite. The reason for the nickname isn't as bad as you might think. My daddy had the same name as my grandda before him. As far back as I remember, firstborns were carrying the same name. It was easier to call me Bingo than to call out my name only to have ten people answering you." He grinned. "My name is Parkland James Monroe the—let me think a minute here. Your daddy was the seventeenth, so that makes me the sixteenth. Parkland James Monroe the sixteenth. Can you believe that? My goodness. I wonder what other nicknames were used back along the line."

Elizabeth sat up and stared at him. "You are the sixteenth? My goodness, Grandda, I had no idea. And since my dad didn't have sons, there won't be anyone else called that." He nodded. "That's about the saddest thing I've ever heard. The line ended with Dad."

"Yes. However, it's a long line of Monroe's honey. A great deal longer line than most people ever have. Why I couldn't believe it when we got to name your daddy; everyone thought we were having a little girl. I wouldn't have minded at all. Not really. I was just so happy that he was healthy." She asked him if he had missed him. "I do—every single day. If not for you living with us, I think it might have been harder on your grannie and me. She surely did hurt when your dad and mom passed. I'm so happy we got to keep you with us for as long as we did."

"I am as well. There is no telling what might have happened to me had you not taken me in." He took her hand into his and kissed the back of it. "That's enough sadness today, thank you very much. I'm happy. You're happy, and we'll take what we can for the rest of our days. All right?"

"Sounds like a plan to me, honey. I like that." He asked her about the house and how it was coming along. "I know you two were putting your heads together about some of the rooms. I have to admit; I do like that Robert wanted to combine the rooms, so they were bigger. You don't think about that sort of thing when you're putting up a house. The people who owned it before wouldn't have thought about an inside terlit either."

He'd been calling the toilet a *terlit* since she could remember. It wasn't as if he didn't know what it was called, but he said that his mom called it that and liked it. She thought him goofy but knew if he were still alive when she and Robert had a child, their child would also be calling it that.

For the rest of the afternoon, they talked about the house. He was going to put his on the market when he got out of the hospital, and Sherman, another Archer, was going to help him. However, before he did that, he wanted her to go through the house and take whatever she wanted. Also, he wanted her to have all the photos on the walls and a few albums that her granny had put together.

"I'd like that. Bring some of the things that belonged to you to the house. You're still going to be living with us, right?" He asked her if she was sure about that. "I've never been more sure about anything other than my love for Robert. And he'll be disappointed in you if you don't. I think he plans to learn everything he can from you before you push up some daisies."

"He's a smart boy, that one. I'm betting that before the end of the week, he's got more ideas on running the business than I ever did. Even if he didn't have a lick of training in being a construction worker, he wouldn't let that stop him. As I said, he's a smart boy." She told him that she thought he was too. "Nah, I'm not smart. I have a good head on my shoulders about putting a house up and together, but I don't know squat about how to give people what they want that I'm not used to building. He's already shown me how to put on a deck made of old stones that he found in the yard where we park the heavy equipment. And there was a pile of slate out there that he insisted was worth some money. He was darned if he wasn't able to sell it off for a good penny too. I'd of just had the boys dump it in the dumpster come winter for them something to do. Other things too. He donated a bunch of things that we've pulled out of houses to the local shelter for them to clean up. A couple of them down there have the skills to make them work like new. Never would have thought of that had he not told me."

"He and his family have been at it, selling things for people for a while, I guess. And it's good to be able to clean up things that would otherwise end up in a dumpster." He told her that he'd not thought of it that way. "I don't mean just you, Grandda. I'm talking about many projects like that one that they find a way to make it into something else or give it away so that someone else can sell it off."

She walked around the hallways with him when the nurse reminded him to do it. As they moved around the hall, several people stopped them from talking to her grandda. She'd forgotten how social he was and shouldn't have been surprised when everyone knew that he'd not had a stroke but had fallen asleep at the wheel. They also seemed to understand why he'd turned over the company to Robert. Even without the two of them getting married, they told him he still had made an excellent choice. As they made their rounds down the hallway three times, he said he'd had enough of socializing. When they returned to the room, Robert was there waiting. He kissed her and hugged grandda. The two of them acted like they were best friends, and she couldn't be happier.

"I have a job for you to help me with, Bingo. It's the Masterson building. The city wants it torn down. I'm not so sure that's the best route only because I love that old building. They're talking about it being an eye sore, and all I can see is that it's been neglected for the last decade or so. How much work would it take to spruce it up a bit? It's too late to plant flowers or trees, I was told, but I'd hate to see it torn down for another parking lot. That's the plan for it."

"Well, what ideas did you have for the old building? Keep in mind that there isn't much in the way of use for those buildings anymore. They don't have any air conditioning. No way to put it in without costing a bundle. Also, this might not have been a consideration to those folks at city hall, but that building isn't just an eye sore; it's kind of dangerous. If a hard storm came through, it would fall and land on several people. Worse yet, another building. I like that you'd like to preserve the building, but I'm not entirely sure it's worth the money." Robert asked him what he'd do. "Oh, I'd tear it down. But with hanging out with you, I have a good idea. Sell off the bricks. Tell them that the money is going to one of the Christmas funds. I know that I'd like to have a couple of them. Just on account of my misses and me got married in that place."

"I love that idea, grandda. And it would benefit many people too while it's being torn down. Hell, I'm betting there will be many weddings before it's torn down. It would be so romantic to say they were the last to be married there."

"I'm glad to hear you say that." Robert got down on one knee and proposed to Elizabeth again. Bingo was so glad that he was a part of it; he didn't bother wiping at the tears when they started to fall. Robert looked over at him. "We're to be married in the morning at the old building. My family will be there, and my brother will release you if you promise to behave and have someone else drive you there, Bingo."

"You bet that I will. I've got a granddaughter to be giving to you, young man. And you'd best be on your best behavior too." He was still laughing when they left to get dinner for the three of them. Bingo was happy. Happier than he'd been in quite some time, as a matter of fact.

Chapter 4

Lance watched his sister as she worked on the wedding dress. She came in at night, which was fine by him to have a quiet place to work. He would hang out with her until she was ready to go home and he'd take her back then go onto his job. Lance didn't want anything to happen to her while she was here alone.

It was her shop; he supposed that she could do anything she wanted. When she was at the stand that held the dress, he asked her if she wanted anything to drink. He was suddenly not just thirsty but a little hungry too.

"No, I'm fine. I have water and snacks in the fridge under my desk if you want anything." He said he'd get something in a little while. "All right. Just be quiet.

I need to have quiet time to work on all these beads. I know that's difficult for you, but just try and refrain from telling me every little detail about your day." He told her that he'd try, laughing with her.

She was good at what she did. And she loved it. Making wedding dresses for the rich was something that she'd done since she'd been a child, and making them for her dolls. Mom had done it as well with the two of them in bed; she'd create masterpieces that would keep them in bread in milk, she used to say. It had done a good deal more than that. They'd been wealthy since he'd been just a child. The only thing that they lacked in was love. Hugs had never been given, nor a kiss on the cheek. Their parents weren't demonstrative at all.

Going into Lannie's office, he got himself a bottle of water and a couple of the snack packs they'd had as children for their lunches. Eating the pudding, he thought it had an off taste and picked up the package to see what flavor it was. Dizzy now, he stood up to go to his sister when he heard voices. He never got to her as he passed out from whatever he was sure was in the pudding.

Waking up, he was on the floor of the office. Somehow he'd ended up under her desk and behind her filing cabinet. Sitting up carefully, unsure if he'd been hurt or only poisoned, Lance dragged his body up from the floor, holding onto the desk for a few moments to get his head to stop spinning. Leaning back down was difficult, but he put the pudding cups that he'd been eating on the ledge at the back of her desk. He had no idea why that seemed important, but he was a cop, after all. Going into the room where his sister had been working, he realized a couple of things. It was bright in the room, so it had to be morning, he'd bet, and Lannie wasn't at the dress.

Hoping that she'd taken a nap on her sofa, he turned to see if she was there. She wasn't there, so he looked around. That's when he got a look at the wedding dress. It was covered in blood.

"Lannie? Lannie? Where are you?" Staggering to the stool she'd been sitting on when he'd left her, he saw that the dress was bloodied and a significant amount on the floor and walls around it. "Lannie? Please tell me where you are."

"Here." He made his way to her soft voice and found his sister. Dropping to the floor, he wondered how she was still alive. Lannie looked like she'd been shot a dozen times, and her face was bloodied and beaten. "Call Sherman Archer. He'll know what to do."

"Don't talk. I'm calling for you an ambulance." She

told him it was too late for her. "Don't say that, Lannie. You're all I have."

"I've stayed alive to tell you this, Lance. Call Sherman. Tell him it was Tommy. Promise me, Lance. Promise?" He said that he would. "I love you. So much. I'm sorry that we are going to part like this. You're the best twin that anyone could have ever hoped for."

When she closed her eyes, he cried for her to wake up. Knowing she was gone didn't make him want her to wake up any less. He was dying inside himself. His heart no longer beat the way that it had before. Christ, what was he going to do now, he thought. She had been his reason for making all the decisions in his life. The reason that he wanted to be the best that he could be. He loved her more than he did himself.

Pulling out his cell phone, he called the police station. Telling them where he was, who he was, and that there had been a murder. Giving them the address, he realized that she'd not be coming here again to work. Every little thing about this room and the building surrounding it would forever make him think of his little sister. He was crying again when he closed his cell phone.

Sitting back on his ass, he held her hand while waiting on the first of his men in blue to arrive. Speaking to his sister, all he had in the world as a family, he cried hard, thinking she'd been too young to die.

"When we were little, you used to tell me that you were going to go places. I don't think you ever made it beyond the city limits. So many times, we made plans that were canceled. I wish I'd not let my job interfere with us." He cried harder when her hands, usually so warm, began to chill. "Lannie, what am I supposed to do without you? How will I ever get around now that you're not there to keep me moving? I don't want to go on without you, Lannie. Please, you have to come back to me. Please?"

When the first officer arrived, he didn't move. They all knew his sister. Some of them had even tried to date her. But they were professional about the murder and didn't cut him any slack even though he was their boss. The medical team arrived shortly after the first officers did. There was nothing they could do to bring Lannie back, but that didn't stop them from trying. They, too, knew his sister as she volunteered weekly at the station house to cook them meals when she didn't have a deadline, which wasn't all that often. But she continued to make time for them.

"Did you see the killer, Lance?" He told Ben about

the pudding that he'd eaten. But didn't mention the cups that he'd hidden away with the water bottle. "We'll send it to the lab. Also, you'll need to get to the hospital so that we can get some results back."

"You have to arrest me, Ben. I'm here with my sister. I know you don't want to, but you have to." He looked away, then back at him. "I'm going to find who killed her. I promise you that. She made me promise—I have to make a phone call. Can I do that first?"

"I'll make it for you. I don't know who it is, but you don't want to make a call, and it comes up as questionable. All right?" He told him that was good thinking on his part. "She was the light of everyone's life, Lance. I don't…I can't imagine why anyone would want to murder her. And so violently too. She was one of the best."

Lance started crying again. His heart was broken, and he didn't think that it would ever beat again without his sunshine in his life. When they took her away, still working on trying to save her, Lance sat in the chair offered to him while the medical team took blood samples and checked him over. Once they finished with him ensuring them that he was all right, they put him in a cruiser to take him to the jail cell for now. He didn't care where they took him at this point. He just wanted to go to the hospital where she was. Hold her a bit more. The closer he was to Lannie, the better he'd feel anyway.

Lannie was his younger sister by eight minutes. But to others, his police family, they thought her older simply because she seemed to have a good head on her shoulders. Mostly it was because she'd scold him about his eating habits—which were very poor—and his inability to keep a girlfriend. It brought a small smile to his face when he thought of the conversation they'd had recently.

"What about you? You make pretty dresses for brides, yet you date less than I do." She told him that she'd seen what couples are genuinely like and wanted no part of it. "Not all couples are like our parents, love. You have to know that."

"I'm sure there are more parents and couples like them than you think. Besides, who will tell your future wife what sort of person you are? Me, that's who." They often bantered back and forth like that. For hours, it seemed. But neither of them got upset, nor did they leave without a long hug and telling each other that they loved them. The phone was handed to him by Ben. After saying his name, the man on the other end started talking.

"I don't know who this is, but I'm about to go into the courtroom to hear a case I don't want anything to do with. Either tell me why I shouldn't just hang up on you, or I will do just that." He told him that he was Lannie Jacobson's brother, Lance. "Lannie? Christ, I've not heard from her — what's going on that you're calling me?"

"She's dead." Lance broke down. He was sobbing to the stranger about how she was gone and that her last words were for him to call him. To tell him that Tommy had done it. "She was murdered, and now I'm all alone, Mr. Archer. What the hell am I going to do without her?"

"Listen to me, Lance. Have they taken you to the hospital?" He said that they'd taken him to jail. "Good. Stay there until you hear from me. I have to make a couple of calls but do not allow anyone to put an IV in you nor to take any of your blood."

"They did that at the scene. What's going on that has you telling me this like I'm guilty?" He said that he wasn't guilty and that he didn't want him to end up that way. "I didn't kill my sister, Mr. Archer. I couldn't have done that—"

"I'm sorry. But listen to me, Lance. Don't allow anyone to take your blood. I don't want you to answer any questions, say nothing about anything. You were on scene, I take it?" Lance told him everything, including the part about the pudding. "I'll get someone to the shop to find the one you ate out of. Do you know where it might be?"

"It was under the desk where I was. I put it away so that it wouldn't be obvious as to where it was. I didn't know that Lannie was…I didn't know about Lannie at that time. Also, you need to be aware that there are cameras all over her shop. They have a recorder in the offices, but everything is automatically uploaded to some kind of offsite place. It uploads every twenty-four hours with not just the time stamped but the date and year as well." He asked for and was given the sign-in and the password to get them. Sherman told him not to say anything to the officers about it. "I won't. You're kind of scaring me. These are my men. I don't think they'd do anything like this to me."

"Do you know who Tommy is, Lance?" All he knew about it was that his sister was afraid of him. "With good reason. I'll explain everything when I get there. I'm having my secretary make some calls. You keep your mouth shut and your fluids where they are now."

~*~

Robert got off the plane in New Orleans at noon.

He thought he'd done well since Sherman had called him only three hours ago to get his ass there. Robert also had a list of things he had to do for Lance. First and foremost, he was going there to talk to the other man. He was arriving just as a lunch tray was being served to him. For the third time, it seemed.

"Lance, you're supposed to eat this. The doc said that you need to eat every bite of it." Lance, he supposed it was the man sitting on the cot, didn't say a word. "Come on now. If I take this back, they're going to make me bring it back to you again. That guy taking over for you while you're here has a real hardon for you to eat this."

"Excuse me. My name is Robert Archer, attorney. I'm here to speak to my client. As for the meal, he just lost his only sister, and I doubt very much I'd want to eat either. Leave it here, and I'll take care of it." The officer, Crumble, his name tag said he was to make sure that Lance ate it. "As I have said to you, I'm here to talk to my client, and you leave it here, and I'll take care of it."

After handing the tray off to him, Robert set it on the floor and took samples of everything on the tray. Once he had them in evidence bags, he sealed them up and put them in his briefcase. He didn't know if he'd make it out of the building with them, but he was curious as to why they wanted him to eat.

"My name is Robert Archer. My brother Sherman sent me here as your representative in this case. How are you feeling?" He said he was dead inside. "I can well imagine. I'm profoundly sorry for your loss. I'm here to make a few things happen for you."

"My sister was murdered. Your brother said he'd explain a few things to me when he arrived. Is he coming?" Robert told him that he was, but not until tomorrow. He was working on things to help him not be arrested. "You think they will? Arrest me, I mean?"

"Yes. I'm going to get you out of here within the next half hour. They've not charged you with anything, and there is no evidence to say that you had anything to do with the murder of your sister." He said they could hold him for twenty-four hours. "Not in this case. I've made a few calls on your behalf, and you will be released in my custody as soon as I can get my wife here. She's a ball buster and will have you a hot cooked meal that I'm sure hasn't anything in it as well as the hospital taking some samples of our own. Did they tell you that your blood came back with amphetamines in them? Also, that it was matched to the blood that they found under her nails. I'm not sure how that is remotely possible as no one has done the autopsy as yet."

"No. They've not said anything to me. Other than to eat and that I had to consent to having my blood drawn. It was too demanding on their part. Even if your brother hadn't told me not to give them any, I think I would not have done it." He said he was a smart man. "Thanks. What about my sister? I need to go and make arrangements for her. I'm sure that she's put them someplace, but I'm not thinking straight right now."

Elizabeth came down the hall with two officers. They were both frowning, and he wondered what had happened. She hugged the man as soon as they unlocked the door to allow Lance to come out.

"I'm putting you a gun in the back of your pants. Cover it up before we step into the hall." Robert looked at the two men with them and noticed that one wasn't carrying a gun. He'd bet any amount of money that the man had given up his weapon for his boss. "All right, Lance, let's go and get you lunch and have a nice long conversation about the things you need to take care of. But first, let me tell you how profoundly sorry I am for your loss. My heart goes out to you."

They were near the front of the station house when

one of the men he'd seen earlier came from Lance's office. He knew it was his because it had his name on the door. The man stepped in front of them as they reached for the door.

"I need your passcode for getting into your computer," Robert asked the man why. "Well, now, this is police business. Nothing to do with you being a suit."

"Have you fired Chief Jacobson? Relieved him from his duties? For that matter, have you charged him with anything?" The man said not yet. "Well, until that time, I'm sure that he'd like to keep his passcode to himself. As his attorney, I'm going to have to advise him not to tell you that."

"Now ain't you all fancy." The man looked at Lance. "Don't you want to solve the murder of your dear sister? I need to get some information from your computer; it has a lock code. Take that off before I have to arrest you."

"For not sharing my passcode with you? I don't believe that will stand up in court, Mr. Mayor. And you could have just asked me if you wanted any information. But now you've put me on the defense. So no, I'm not going to share my passcode with you. Under any circumstances. Now, if you don't mind, I'm ready to have lunch with my attorney."

"We did give you some lunch, but you refused to eat it. That's not very nice of you." Lance said nothing but moved out the door in front of Elizabeth. Robert asked him what was in the meal that had been brought to him. "In it? I haven't any idea what you're talking about. It was just a meal. We just want to keep him healthy enough to stand trial."

"You go on thinking that." As soon as he was out the door, Robert knew that this man was somehow involved in the death of Lannie Jacobson. Proving it might not be as difficult as he thought it might be. The way they showed themselves with all the hostility toward Lance had him thinking that this went deeper than he or Sherman thought. They were all working on this for them.

They headed to the first restaurant that they came to. There wasn't much in the way of people; most tourists were out and about since it was a lovely afternoon. But he wanted someplace quiet and private. This place had both for them. As soon as he was seated, he called the hospital to speak to Doctor James Cumberland.

"Have you had any trouble?" The man laughed. "I'm taking that as a no. Or, since I don't know you well, it could be that you've had trouble and have taken care of it. Which is it?"

"No trouble. However, I did get all the things done that you asked for before anyone showed up. I acted like I'd just gotten here and was ready to start. They had a list of things that they wanted me to look for. Stupid things that I just ignored. Oh, and I'm to give them all the samples I took from the girl. My goodness, Robert, they did a number on this child. She must have suffered badly before passing on."

Robert glanced at Lance, and he nodded for him to go on. He asked if he could put it on speaker phone, and Doctor Cumberland said it was fine by him. The conversation started with Cumberland telling him how sorry he was for his loss.

"Thank you," Cumberland asked if they were in a good place. Lance seemed confused, but Robert clarified for him. "I have a few things that I need to discuss with you that I'd just as soon not have spoken all over the place."

"Yes, we're good here. Just don't be so loud." They all laughed. Cumberland had a very booming voice. "I've gotten the pudding cup that you ate from. It was found under the desk that you'd been lying under. I do believe that's the only reason that you're alive now, young man. No one knew that you were there with her. Everything was handed over to me earlier this afternoon. I'm sending it to the lab that was recommended to me by your mother, Robert. My goodness, she has some strings that are far-reaching, doesn't she? Anyhow, that, along with the things on my end, was picked up by Secret Service just about an hour ago. They said that I'd have results by the end of the day. What I can tell you so far. The clippings from her nails are also in that bundle I was to send out. The police force in this town has taken her clothing. I did manage to get some pieces of it before it was taken out. Blood, tissue as well as the other forensic items were sealed by the notary that you sent here to help me out."

"What was her cause of death?" Lance said he knew it would only be a guess, but he'd like to know. "I mean, I'd never hold you to that. I just need to know. Also, how long did she suffer before I got to her?"

"There could be any number of reasons for her death. Blood loss. Blunt force trauma. Also, she'd been shot eleven times by what appears to me as three different weapons. I have sent all the bullets on with the other things. The police that were here didn't even ask for them.

Lance, I'm sorry, son, but she suffered badly. I'd say that they were with her for at least an hour, perhaps two. I don't know if she was being treated that way for a reason, but I do believe they didn't get whatever it was they wanted. I don't know why but I have a feeling that she took whatever they wanted to the grave." Lance thanked Cumberland, but Robert could tell that it affected him badly to know that she suffered. "Did you say that you thought they were looking for something, Robert? That someone had tossed the room badly?"

"That's what we were able to determine when we looked over the footage of the murder." Robert looked at Lance. "You have any idea what they might have been looking for? I mean, was there a safe or any other means to hide something away?"

"Yes. She had a safe in the room. I never thought to tell you about it before." He wrote down the combination and handed it to Elizabeth when she asked for it. "You shouldn't go there alone, Mrs. Archer. Those people, whoever they are, they won't hold back because you're a woman. No matter how pretty you are."

"I'm not going there alone. But I do thank you for not telling me that I was too female to handle myself. I'm taking my mother-in-law. She's Katherine Archer."

Lance sat back in his chair and stared at the two of them. "I see you know who she is."

"You'd have to be deaf, dumb and stupid not to have — Christ, you're her son. I never, until this moment, put it together who she was. No wonder Lannie said you'd do her right when we talked about things." Lance laid his head on the table and began to cry again. "She's gone. Whenever I think about her, I have to remind myself that she's really gone."

The two of them waited on Lance to gather himself up. When their lunch arrived — they'd not ordered yet — Robert looked at the waitress bringing it to them and saw her shake her head. Just enough for him to know that they shouldn't eat this. Asking her who had ordered it, she simply took it away without a word. That was when Robert noticed that there was a small slip of paper on the table.

"The station house called in an order, and one of the officers there came to 'fix it' for us. The waitress said that she didn't know what was in it but said not to eat anything that she didn't bring us." Lance asked why she'd even brought it. "Apparently, they told the cook that you were suffering terribly after the death of your sister, and they were afraid that you'd try something like killing yourself. She said that it was put in all the meals, whatever it was."

Elizabeth said she'd be back. When she took her black bag with her, Robert knew that the shit was about to hit the fan. When she returned some minutes later, she had a huge grin on her face and told them that the restaurant would be closing soon as the cook and the officer that had doctored the meals were now lying out on the floor.

"I made them taste the food. It wasn't difficult because, apparently, the cook thought it was only a sedative. The officer was a little harder to convince." Lance laughed and asked her if they were going to be all right. "I don't really care, do you? Our waitress is leaving now and won't return. I've given her a nice tip to help her get out of town."

Robert didn't ask. He knew his new wife, as of yesterday morning, would have given her enough to not just start fresh, but she'd bet there was enough money to get a lovely home, too, should she want it.

They talked over the case, the things that they had done in the name of getting him free. Since he'd not been arrested nor charged, they decided that he might be a bit safer in Ohio rather than where they were now. The long arms of the people wanting him to go down for the murder of his sister were starting to stretch out beyond what he thought was smart.

While they were leaving, a limo pulled up in front of the now closed restaurant. It was the Vice President. With him was the courier that had picked up the things that had been left at Lannie's shop as well as the things that he'd gotten from the safe. Without a word, the young man got out of the limo and walked away. As soon as the car started up again, his mom slipped into the car with them as they were pulling away.

"Gilbert, I'm so happy that you could help us out with this. This is a terrible thing they've done to this young family." Gilbert Jamieson told her it was his pleasure. "Be that as it may, you've no idea how much I appreciate this. What have you found out? I'm sure that it's plenty."

"Oh yes, ma'am. More than I think we thought we'd get when I was asked to get the information for you. Mr. Jacobson, did you know that your sister had ties with the president? That she had not only designed his daughter's wedding dress when she married recently but that she was also the go-to person that his wife went to when she needed a gown? My goodness. The things that you can find out when you are looking for clues."

After explaining the things that he found out, Robert was sure that this was going to be more than he could handle on his own. Not only that, but he was sure that all his brothers together were going to be in over their heads with this case. Not only did it have the mayor of the town involved, but it seemed as if every council member in the entire state had something to do with what happened to Lannie Jacobson. Tying it all together was going to be a nightmare without help on how to make sure they didn't lose this case. Because if they did, they'd be in as much shit as the people that were actually involved in all this.

"I'm going to help with the case." Robert asked Gilbert what he insisted on them calling him. "I'm an attorney. I keep up with the things going on. You're going to need a Federal attorney on your team because of the people involved. I'm going to help."

"All right." They all laughed at Robert. "I was just thinking that we'd be in over our heads if we were to try this case on our own. There are laws being broken here that are well above my paygrade."

"We'll get this. The president will be very disappointed in me if we lose this case, young man. I don't want to make that man upset with me, do you?" He and Lance both shook their heads. Mom just huffed. "Katie, I think he's terrified of you more than he is most leaders in other countries. He'd just tell you that you did a good job and take his frustrations out on me. He loves you too."

"And I both of you. But we're not going to lose this case, young man. If we do, then you won't have to worry about the President. I'll take you down a couple of pegs." Gilbert told his mom that he believed her. "And well you should. All right. Let's get you home, Lance. After, we'll run by the funeral home and make some arrangements. Also, I believe that we need to get some blood samples from you as well."

And just like that, they were working on getting Lance out of the state as well as helped. Robert loved his family. Especially his mom. When Elizabeth kissed him on the cheek, he knew that he couldn't have been happier than he was at that moment.

Chapter 5

Robert wasn't a part of the team that was at the table for the defendant. They only allowed a few to sit at what a lot of attorneys he knew called the big boy table, and he'd opted out so that he could keep an eye on the players. He also got to sit by his mom and Elizabeth while William and Sherman had drawn the longest straws. Literally, what they'd done to figure out who was going to be sitting with Gilbert Hamilton, the VP who was the lead in all this mess.

They'd prepared for a week before the attorney for the state of Louisiana had filed that Lance was guilty of murdering his sister. How anyone could have said that after spending ten minutes with the man was a mystery.

The attorney for the other side, the state of Louisiana, didn't look all that thrilled with being at any table, much less the one with the mayor and the governor there with her. As soon as the judge, a Federal Judge, because of the VP being there, was seated, Gilbert stood up.

"Your honor, I'd like a moment of your time, please, in private." He told him he was currently busy at the moment. "Yes, I can see that I have the utmost respect for you taking on this trial on such short notice, but I have only just uncovered something that I should make you aware of."

"Will it make this go a bit quicker, Gilly? I have to tell you, being pulled from my retirement isn't anything that I was happy about." Gilbert told him that he understood, but it would only take a moment if he'd just do this in his office. "That important, is it? Well, let's get this over with. I won't be happy if I have to be coming out here and telling everyone that we're going to be here for weeks at a time. Not one bit."

"I hope that it doesn't come to that either, sir." While huffing all the way to his room, Gilbert asked Ms. Avery Porter if she'd join them. "I want to be clear and upfront on this for all the people involved, Ms. Porter. If you'd like to come with us, I think this will clear a great many things up for your client."

She simply stared at him for a moment or two, then she glanced at William. The two of them had been bickering since William showed up with mismatched shoes. He didn't know why it bothered her more than it did his brother, but he was good-natured about a lot of things, and she just seemed like a bitch.

William was asked to go in with them, as was he. Robert knew the passwords without having to fumble through them, and William was the person who had been decided to explain what was going on with the recordings of not just the night that Lannie had been killed. It appeared that it was also a great many previous nights when Lannie had been working alone in her shop. It was going to get messy quickly, he thought. As soon as they were in the office of the judge, Ms. Porter started talking.

"This is preposterous. First, we're rushed along on this trial. I'm barely given anything other than the barest of facts." Robert stared at her with an open mouth. "I don't want to be here, judge. For all the reasons that I gave you in my letter of resignation from this trial. I think the opposing party should know I'm here under duress."

"I'm sure they got that you didn't want to be here when you told your client to shut his mouth and not to open it again. Ms. Porter, can you tell me what it is that has you so fired up about this case?" She told him that she'd put it in her letter. "Yes, but since you've been so honest so far, why don't you simply spill the beans on what you told me. We're all friends here." She huffed before speaking.

"I think that all of them are guilty, and I can't, not with good conscience, give them my best when I dislike every one of the fuckers. Since we're being honest. I didn't know Lannie Jacobson, but from what I've been able to find on my own, she was an incredible woman that didn't deserve this. I read the shit that they gave me, and it's all lies. Every single word of it." The judge nodded and looked at William. She turned as well. "Mr. Mismatch here is going to lose if he doesn't get his act together and—"

"I've had about enough of you talking to me as if I'm an imbecilic. I graduated at the top of my class at Harvard. I have a doctorate in law, which I hate doing anymore. Mostly because of clients like yours. I want to do things that please me, not things that make me feel as if I have to shower after every meeting with my client. But this case is different. This man, Lance Jacobson, is one of the good guys. Since I've met him, he's been nice, kind and wonderfully attentive to not just my elderly grandda but to my mom as well. You, however, are a bitch. Yeah, I said it, and if you don't get off my wearing the wrong shoes today, I'm going to have a word or two to say to your boss about your integrity."

"I'm quitting as soon as this sham of a trial is over." He told her that was probably the smartest thing she'd said all day. "Thanks. I think." She looked at the judge. "Can we get this over with?"

The small device she took out of her pocket looked like a recorder. Before he could begin to question why she was wearing it, she picked up the statue that was on the desk and smashed it. No one said a word about it, and she sat down. Robert stood up. Then he sat down. Looking at his brother William when he stood up as well, they both looked at Avery.

"What? I didn't give them anything. That's what they want, you know. To see what you have so that they can get rid of it or the people you're using. That's only one of the reasons that I want nothing to do with these people. They're corrupt, and I don't want to go down with them. Or, what I think is going to happen, they're going to blame it all on me somehow and get my ass in prison. Also, your boy out there. They want him dead too." William told her that they knew that. "I thought you might. All right. Let's see what you have for me to work with so that I can go out there and tell someone that they need to plead guilty or face prison time."

"All of them." She smiled at Gilbert when he spoke. "No, I mean all of them are going to go to prison. From the governor to just about every mayor in this area. And all for what Lannie knew."

They were perhaps about five minutes into the first recording when the mayor stuck his head into the room. How he was able to do that was beyond him, but there he stood. Gilbert sat down on the device that Avery had crushed so that whomever it was, they'd not see it.

"Hello. I'm sorry. I need to speak to my attorney." No one moved, especially not Avery. It was then that he noticed that William had a tight hold on her jacket. "Avery, will you please step out here for a moment. I think we have an issue."

"We don't, but you might want to come on in here and have yourself a listen." Everyone turned to the judge. "Robert, go out there and get that moron of a governor too. Might well get this finished up before we have to waste any taxpayers' money, don't you think?"

The room was crowded now, and the stenographer

suggested that they clear out the courtroom and have the meeting in there. After making a quick call, not only was the room opened up for them, but there were Secret Service officers all around the room as well. At every doorway and window. Gilbert blew them off as being there for him. He was the VP, after all.

"All right now. We're going to all keep our mouths shut and listen to this recording." Robert told him that he could set it up to be able to be watched as well if they had a sheet or two to show it on. "I can do you one better than that. Just down the hall is a projector that works with computers as well as a large screen. I did some digging while I was here yesterday. You set it up, Robert, and we'll have us a show. I'll even send out for some popcorn while we're at it."

In the end, after setting it all up, lunch was ordered for them all. Robert had a feeling it was to keep everyone close to them. William pulled him aside while they were waiting on their meals.

"I've given the officers in here a list of the mayors that have been involved in all this when I was asked. I think they're sending someone there to have them arrested. I still wonder where Lannie might have gotten that book from. Do you suppose she stole it?" Robert told him that she'd given her life for it, so it mattered little to him where she'd gotten it. "That's very true. I guess she didn't know who to trust, did she?"

"Would you?" William shook his head and looked at Avery. "What are you thinking about her? That she might well be playing us? To be honest with you, I don't think that she is. She is really upset about all this."

"She's like the others." It took him a minute to figure out what he was saying about the other women in the family. "I'm not saying that I want her in my life, not even if she were to be my sister-in-law. I can't stand her, but I trust her. I don't know why but I do."

"That's good enough for me." The food was delivered in record time. While they were eating, no one talked but the mayor and the governor, and several messages were given to the judge. "I can't for the life of me remember if I ever heard his name, the judge, I mean. Usually, I can look up on the dais and remember it that way, but it's not there."

"Federal Judge Samuel Haas. I believe that mom knows him and is the one that asked him to come here and sit this one." He didn't know why but he wasn't surprised that his mom would have known the man. "She told him that some shaky shit was going on, and she wanted someone that she could trust here so that her boys, us, wouldn't be going to prison for helping out the country."

"Thank god she's on our side." They both laughed. "Avery is avoiding them all. I don't blame her at all, but she is going to be in a world of hurt if they don't arrest these people today. Understand what I mean?"

"Yes. She's not helping us, not really, but I know that she will if it comes to that. Also, did you notice that the mayor gave her the eye when she came out of the room and walked away from him? Do you think he knows what she said in there and that she destroyed the recording thing she had on her?" Robert could only nod as the mayor came to sit with them.

He didn't speak to either of them, but he did keep an eye on them. Like he wasn't hiding the fact that he was wondering what they were talking about. It looked like he was going to ask them when Judge Haas asked him to get things finished up to watch the recording. Robert was shocked when Judge Haas pointed to the recording of the night of the murder. He did so and then sat back down by his brother. He could almost repeat every word that had been said that night.

"What are you doing here, David? I thought that

you agreed to stay out of my life or else." The mayor was David Sorrel, he remembered now. Lannie spoke again as she stood up and turned toward the two men. "Tommy? You're here too? Must be a big night for the two of you to be out after dark."

"Wait a fucking minute here. Just wait a fucking minute. Where the hell did you get this tape?" Judge Haas told him that he'd better be sitting down and shutting up. "I will not. They doctored this up so that it looks like me and my nephew were there. I won't have it. Avery? Get up off your ass and object to this?"

"Object to what? They're only playing the recording of the night that Ms. Jacobson was killed. Why do you care? You told me that you weren't involved, didn't you? Said you weren't there. If you're not lying to me, then sit down like you were told." Avery stood up when Sorrel walked to her. "You touch me, and I'll show them what you did to me to make me be here today."

He only had a moment to wonder about that when Sorrel laughed. "Your little girl is going to be all right, Avery. So long as you play with the grown-ups." She looked around Sorrel, and he turned. There was a SS man standing behind him. "No need for you to get your drawers all bunched up, sir. We're just having a friendly—"

"He threatened her." Everyone turned to look at William. "I believe he also has her daughter too. I'm not sure about that, but I'd say that's a good guess. Does he have her, Avery?"

Tears formed in her eyes as she nodded. However, before anyone asked her to say it aloud that he did indeed have her, Sorrel was on the floor with a gun at the back of his head. It took a shot to his shoulder, which surprised the hell out of him to get him to tell them where she was.

"Tommy has her. The fucker said he'd take good care of her." The Servicemen, Army, Robert thought, that seemed to appear out of nowhere, got the address and left as a unit. "You're going to pay for this, Avery. You'll never work as an attorney anywhere again. I'll see to that personally."

"Good luck with that, moron." Avery thanked William and then turned to the judge. "I have a lot of shit to get cleaned up before this moron is out of here. Can we please get this show on the road so that I can go to my little girl?" |

"Yes. I'll have them bring her here for you. After she goes to the hospital." Judge Haas stood up. "If there is one hair on her head out of place, I'll tear you apart. On that, you can bank. Get this started, Robert. I suddenly feel nasty all over my body."

Sorrel was jerked up from the floor laughing. As soon as he was put in a chair and handcuffed, the laughter stopped. He looked at the screen that he'd been playing the recording on. There wasn't going to be any doubt that the two men standing there with Lannie were anyone but him and his nephew Tommy. They had their guns out and pointed at her when he paused it.

~*~

Elizabeth checked out young Penny. Avery wanted her daughter in her arms, but she was waiting on her to finish with her exam. The hospital had been very accommodating, especially after the president called and told them that Elizabeth could practice anywhere he said she could. And that she'd better be treated like he was there talking to them. Katie, who had been at the hotel with her this morning, was talking to the nurse about the weather while Avery and she watched Penny.

"I did what you told me to do, mom." Avery, still on the verge of tears whenever her daughter spoke, nodded. "He didn't stand a chance once I found the iron pipe. Hitting him in the balls and then in the head while he was down wasn't fair play, and I know you like only fair play, but he took me right out of my bed when I was sleeping. Mom, I don't want that stuff in my room anymore either."

"All right. I don't think I'd want it, either. We'll get you something completely different." Avery was finally able to touch her daughter when Elizabeth stepped back. "I was terrified for you, honey. My heart nearly stopped beating when I didn't find you in your bed the other morning. I want you to know that I was going to do whatever they told me so that I could get you back."

Penny was nearly ten. She'd told them that every time they said she was nine. But unlike other nine year olds that she knew, this kid was smart. Not just book smart but street smart too. Her mother had taught her how to defend herself, hide and how to get out of a bad situation. When the two of them seemed to be finished hugging, for the moment anyway, it was Katie that asked the questions.

"You hit this grown man with a pipe, then cuffed him to the chair that he had you in. May I ask you how you got out of the cuffs?" She handed a pretty little ring to Katie. "I don't understand."

"It's a cuff key. Mom wears one too. I'll show you how it works." After flipping the rose that was the center of the ring upward. A key was there. "It's made from a real key too. Mom knows some guy who makes them for young women who are on their own. But when dummy cuffed me to the chair, I waited until he was sleeping or high, I can't tell the difference, but when he was out, I uncuffed myself and found me a weapon. Mom told me that all the planning in the world won't help you if you're stupid enough to go back in the house where the killer was without something to defend yourself with. So I waited for him to wake up and beat the snot out of him."

"The Army showed up just as she was leaving the building. After making each one of them show her some identification, she took them back into the building to get Tommy. He was out cold with a concussion. He's been arrested for kidnapping for now. The rest will come as soon as they get him stitched up." Robert kissed her on the mouth and then kissed his mom on the cheek. "The men that were there to save you are so impressed with what you did that you'll be all around the world about your bravery once they're back on base."

"Gee, that's neat. I did what my mom told me. Well, one of the things she told me. Another one is telling people to back off first. If they don't, then I've done my part in having to hurt them when they don't do what I tell them." Elizabeth laughed with Robert. "Also, this is really important. I have to make sure that she knows when I'm going to be in trouble at school. I get that way sometimes when the teacher says things that aren't true about me and my mom."

"Like what?" Robert seemed to be enjoying the little girl and sat down in one of the chairs that were in the room. "I would think that your teacher would be a little afraid of you and your mom."

"Oh, she is now. Last month I got sent home because some boy was pulling on my hair, and I put up a fuss to him to the teacher. Bobby, the boy, said that it needed to be off my neck so that he could see it better. I didn't understand that, so I asked my mom. She told me that it was sexual harassment." Elizabeth asked Penny what grade she was in. "I'm a senior in high school. I have a very brilliant brain. Anyway, after I went to school the next day, he did it again. I asked him if he thought my ten year old neck was going to give him a hard-on. He was so embarrassed that he slapped me. After that, he was suspended for a month and not able to play football for the rest of the school year. Which is very bad on his part. He's a good player when he's not been an idiot, and no one will see him in his senior year. Oh well. I had to get three stitches in my mouth for it. No one believed him when he told them what I said to him. And I didn't say anything either."

Robert laughed. So did she, but Robert looked like he was losing it after the kid told him what she'd done. He finally asked her if she was always so straightforward. When she nodded, her mom told her to use her words. The kid didn't seem to have any trouble with that rule either.

"I don't want to brag, but I have a very good vocabulary. I sometimes have to talk down to adults because they don't believe that I know and understand the words that I'm using. Teachers have the worse time with me about it. If they make fun of me, I simply talk over their heads until they get frustrated with me and send me to the office. The Spanish and French teachers, which is what I'm taking as an elective, hate when I'm in their class because I can speak several languages without any trouble." Katie asked her if she was planning to go to college. "Yes. That's what I want to do. I've been applying at different ones, but I'm having trouble getting anyone to give me a recommendation. They don't like me much, I guess."

It didn't really seem to bother the young girl that no one liked her. If that was true. But Elizabeth had an idea that Katie was going to take care of that for her. Either she'd write her one, or she knew a few people that would do it. William joined them in the room when his mom stepped out to finish her calls.

"I've just spoken to Haas. He said that with all the tampered blood work that he's gotten as well as the things from Elizabeth, they're going to charge both Tommy and Sorrel with witness tampering as well as the attempted murder of Penny. There are other charges as well, but I thought those would be the ones that you'd want to know about first. Seventeen mayors or their equivalent have been arrested and charged with a pleather of items on the book that Lannie had. Oh, you asked me how she ended up with the book. I asked Lance. He said that she told him that she'd been in the office one day and found it out in the open. I don't think that he believed her." Robert asked him what he thought had happened. "Lance believes that she was raped and beaten by Tommy or both him and Sorrel. Lannie was forever telling him that she was clumsy, but he figured out that she was being hurt. The reason that he'd go to the shop with her when she went there alone. There is no way for us to know for sure now."

"No, I guess not. But I was wondering why she didn't go to the police sooner and was told that she didn't have anyone to trust. She'd been terrified that someone would hold her brother for it." It was Elizabeth who asked why they'd not done that. "They never told anyone that they were related. It wasn't in any of Lance's paperwork. And she wasn't the next of kin on his life insurance policy. Lannie and Lance were never together unless it was at the shop. They only thought that she had hired him to keep an eye on her. As for the puddings and water, they were all laced with fentanyl. I guess they weren't taking any chances that she didn't get the right one. The one that Lance ate and threw up, it was just lucky for him that he'd gotten most of it out of his belly and that he was a strong, healthy man. Otherwise, this might not have ever been solved."

Elizabeth found that to be not just scary but sad as well. From everything that she'd heard about the two of them, they were about the nicest people ever. It's a real shame that she had to die so young and so violently so that some ass wipes thought that they were better than anyone else could get away with murder.

She didn't want to release Penny just yet, but she

knew that Avery would feel better if she had her at home. However, it was William that suggested that they go to a hotel until the new force that was at the stationhouse could go over her place. Almost as soon as both of them agreed it might be a better idea than going back to a tainted home, Sherman called.

"I have some paperwork here that I need to have signed by Avery and her daughter. The state representative is giving them a reward for figuring this out for the state. Also, mom made a few calls, and there will be a letter of recommendation at the hotel for Penny from the President for her to use as a recommendation for her college entrance. He also is making sure that she has a full ride to any place she wants to go in the United States." Penny squealed with delight, and her mom seemed shell-shocked. "Also, I will need to talk to Lance. There is some money coming to him as well. Also, a recommendation for him to not go back to work at the station. I'm going to see if we can get him to come to Ohio with us and run our department. It needs a good man like him."

"Great idea." Elizabeth was excited for all of the men in her family. "Maybe we can talk Avery and her daughter to come out for a long visit too while we're at it. Just to be away from all the crap that has been going on around here."

"Yes. I'd love that." There was no hesitation on Avery's part about saying that was what she wanted to do. Elizabeth didn't know why she agreed so readily but was happy for all of them. "Penny and I talked it over when I came here, and there is very little at the house that we want. It's all been dirtied, and neither one of us what any memories of the night she was taken from me."

Going to dinner at the hotel seemed the best way to get them all together. There wasn't much they didn't try on the menu, and they shared everything they ordered. When dessert was brought to them, Elizabeth was surprised to see that neither Avery nor Penny ate any of the sweet things. She didn't ask because it wasn't any of her business. But how could anyone turn down Bananas foster? Made right at the table.

Elizabeth and Katie went with Avery to pick up some things they could use at the hotel. She was serious about not going back to the house and asked if they could find someone to donate all the furniture as well as linens and such.

"I don't want anything there. A few pictures, of course, and some things that are in the trunk in the attic that were my daughters but the rest of it could burn to the ground for all I care about it." Elizabeth told her that she was sorry for that. "I'm not. We had a good run at the house. It's only a rental, but it was ours. Now it's not. Getting a fresh start will be wonderful for us both. We're looking forward to getting everything set up for us to be a family."

Elizabeth did wonder if she was going to be a part of their family by falling in love with one of the others. But she didn't care. They got along well, as she was sure the rest of the family would as well. It was going to be a good thing to have new people around again.

Chapter 6

Robert had just finished up his day and was sitting on the deck out back. The trees were just beginning to get their fall colors. One tree, in particular, was bright with yellows and oranges, while green still was the predominant color. When it swayed in the light breeze, the beautiful leaves would decorate his lawn. Watching the squirrels run around playing some kind of tag in them made him laugh every time he saw them. Robert decided right then and there that he was never raking again.

It had been a month now since the death of his sister, and Lance had been staying with him and Elizabeth. However, just last night, he told them that he was thinking of finding himself someplace on his own. He was still taking it hard that his twin was gone. But after a few weeks now, he was beginning to talk to people that would come over. When he sat down with him on the deck, the two of them watched the animals playing around before Lance turned to him.

"I'm going to go away for a while. I've been thinking about Lannie and my last conversation, and I want to do something for her. She always wanted to see the world. I'm going to take her ashes with me and see the world with her. Leaving a little of her behind each place I take her. What do you think of that?" Robert told him that he loved the idea. "Yeah, me too. I think that she'd love it too. Seeing me get out and about. I've been hurting long enough, she'd tell me to get my ass in gear."

"You're going to come back, right?" Robert watched the other man when he turned to the back of the property again. "Lance? You are going to return to us, aren't you?"

"It was my plan to not return. I'll be honest with you and tell you that my plan was to do this for my sister and end my own life. It's been difficult since I lost her. I was telling myself, convincing myself that I could have saved her had I not eaten the pudding. But Avery came to see me last night. Well, yesterday afternoon. We spent an hour just talking, and then she asked me what my plans were for my sister's shop and her things left there."

"And? I'm assuming that the two of you came to a decision." He nodded, not taking his eyes off the leaves flying up in the air each time one of the squirrels were chased through them. "Lance, you're starting to scare me a bit. You know that your sister is gonna be pissed off if you show up wherever she is dead, don't you?"

"Yes. Avery, who didn't know her at all, told me the same thing." Lance turned to look at him with a smile on his face. "She was a bit more...forceful, I guess you could say. But yes, she told me that Lannie would be pissed off. I've given her the things in the shop. The building is owned by me now, and I'm going to try renting it out. William is going to help me out with that. Avery is going to have the shop packed up and brought here. I guess she has a building in mind here that she wants to work in."

"Will she take over what your sister was doing?" Lance told him what Avery had said to him. "I can see that. There is always a need for someone to tailor a pair of pants or jacket. Also, her being able to alter dresses, even wedding dresses, will keep her busy, I'm thinking."

"She said that she was going to see about putting

some of the dresses that Lannie made out for sale too. There are a great many of them, I believe. I would think that there are about fifty of them that she made and never sold." Robert asked him if he had wanted any of them. "No. I thought about it. Keeping them, but again, that isn't anything that she'd want me to do. Even though she did keep a lot of dresses back for some reason."

They talked about his sister more. It surprised him how much he talked about her flaws as well as her supposed perfection at things. When he laughed at a couple of things that she'd done in her life, Robert enjoyed that as well. When Lance settled back in his chair, quiet for a bit, Robert thought that the man was more on the mend than he'd first thought.

"I'll be back. I don't know when but I will return." Robert thanked him for that. "Coming here is just what I needed. No one has pressured me into getting over her death. There hasn't been a time when someone has walked away from me when I began to sob all over myself about missing her. It's been what I think my sister and I missed growing up. A family. We had our parents, but they weren't anything like the people you have here. I certainly hope that—what am I saying. I know you tell each other you love them every day. It's what's helped me heal and come to terms with my sister's death. The amount of love that you've all shared with me too."

"Thank you for that. I'm glad we were able to help you, but you telling me this, it's made me feel better too." They sat there in silence again. The squirrels had stopped playing, and now there was a family of deer in the yard. They were enjoying the evening as well, it appeared to him. "Bingo is coming over later to tell me that he's moving out. Not completely, but he needs his own space."

"How do you know what he's going to talk to you about?" Robert told him that he'd spoken to his mom and that his mom wanted to prepare him for it. "He is a nice man. I can see where you'd miss having him around. He sure is energetic. More so than I think most of the men that work with the two of you."

"You got that right. He's showing me a great deal about owning and running a construction company. Right now, I'm doing the jobs that he assigns me so that I can get a feel for them. So far, hanging drywall is my favorite. It wasn't at first, but the symmetry of it is what makes me feel good about hanging it. The way that it makes a room be a room. I love the way that it just hangs there, waiting for someone to come along and paint. I don't know. I think it's relaxing now. I don't care for painting. To me, that sort of shows that the room is nearly finished up and that the color was all it was waiting for."

"You really do love your job, don't you?" Robert, slightly embarrassed, told him that he did, actually. "It shows. I used to feel that way about being a cop. Then as I got promoted, the more I was removed from being a cop to someone that would only get to hear about the things that were going on outside my office when I went out to get something for myself. I was talking to the officers here, and they told me that their chief, who is retiring soon, doesn't have an office. And he goes out on calls like they do. I think, if I were to take that job, that is just the way I'd do things. Be a part of it and not be the man who makes out the schedule and assigns jobs."

"That is the very reason that my brothers and I have decided to not be attorneys. I did enjoy it for a while. Being the person who would win a settlement for the underdog. Or win what seemed an unwinnable case. But it became old. My clients were getting stupider. The crimes were worse than any I'd ever thought of. Then you've got the child abusers, sexual deviants and so on. I love it that I can come home from working hard all day, using not just my brain but my muscles as well and sit out here and have a nice conversation with someone that comes out to see me. Elizabeth and I will be out here after dark some nights just enjoying the quiet of the day." He asked him what he'd be doing if he was an attorney. "Working on a case. Looking things up in law books that are older than I am to win. Taking phone calls from people that have gotten too drunk to drive and did it anyway, hit a tree or another car and need me to get them off. It became too much to deal with every day. I need this right here to live longer."

When Elizabeth joined them, Lance got up to leave. After begging him to stay, he said that he had some things that he needed to see to before he left. After he moved into the house, Robert explained to her what Lance had told him.

"Do you think he'll really return?" Robert told her that he did, but it wasn't up to him. But he didn't think that he'd not just not return. He'd have a reason. "I still worry about him. I mean, he is better than he was when we first met him, but he still grieves for Lannie. I wish we could have known her like he did."

"I think that us not knowing her like he did is what helped him. He might not have been able to talk to us about her had we known all the stories that he told us about them as children through adults. I think too that we know her as well as we would have had we been friends because of him." Elizabeth looked at him like she might be upset. "Or I could be wrong."

"You're not. I think you're absolutely brilliant. We might well have known her better, but not like he did. With all her flaws and good humor. Yes, you're right." She got up from the seat that she'd been on and sat on his lap, facing him. "How did I get so lucky as to find you just when I needed you?"

"I'm the lucky one. I have no idea what my life might have been without you in it. I would have been an attorney, for sure. I wouldn't have a job that I do love. Also, a grandda that I adore in Bingo." She kissed him, a lingering kiss that had him wanting so much more. When she lifted her head, he pulled her back for another heated kiss. "While I thoroughly enjoyed that. What was that for?"

"You and I are going to have a baby." He laughed with her, thinking he supposed that since she laughed, it was a joke. "I talked to a colleague of mine, and she did the test and checked me out. We'll have a baby about the end of May to the first part of June. She can't tell right now because, well, the baby is quite large. I'm assuming —"

Robert kissed her again, this time not stopping when she asked him what it was for. Standing her up, he picked her up and swung her around the deck. Then, fearful that he'd hurt them both, he sat her down and got on his knees before her.

"Did I hurt you?" She shook her head and kissed him. "I've never been a father before. What if I screw up?"

"Then your mom will come over here, beat us both to death and take the baby to raise." He asked her if she was joking. "Not really. But I do think that if we were to screw up, there are any number of people around to tell us what we're doing wrong."

"We need to get some books on having a baby." She told him that they'd already made a baby. "No, I mean raising one. I think there are a few of them we can get."

"I'm sure there are millions of them we could get, but we're not going to. As I said, we have a lot of people around that will help us. Avery, even if she never becomes a part of the family, has a child. Your brother Del has, how many, ten?" Robert told her. "Okay, he has three and one on the way. But there are times when it seems like there are more. But I love them. Every one of them. Even Penny, though she is scary smart, don't you think?"

"She is. We were talking about jet fuel this morning, and she blew my mind. But she did save me some money at the new job site. Who knew that someone that is so perfusion in math could tell me, right down to the screw, how much drywall and mud I'd need to finish the room we were working in and be correct." They both laughed, and he kissed her gentler this time. "I love you, Elizabeth Archer. So very much. And I'm so happy that you're going to have our child that I could about bust with happiness."

"And I love you. Very much." They talked about the baby after he picked her up and put her on his lap. This was the perfect ending to his day, and he hoped that it was for her as well. When it was time for them to go to dinner, having been eating late for the last week or two, and he was enjoying that as well. Robert supposed it was because they both worked so late. Him until nearly seven and her getting off at seven-thirty. Life to him was just about perfect today.

~*~

Elizabeth didn't want any lunch today. She was still full from the dinner they'd had last night. Breakfast with all the trimmings was a wonderful thing to have. However, it was one of those meals that seemed to stick with you for days instead of hours. Now all she wanted was a nap. All the carbs, she figured.

They'd made love last night too. Robert had been so tender with her. Kissing her belly several times before he moved up to her breast. He'd also nibbled on her ear lobes, her nipples and her thighs. After massaging every inch of her legs, he nipped at her skin until he was at her pussy. Christ, the man could win awards by the way he deliciously ate at her.

With his tongue and his fingers, he could and would make her come five or six times straight. Just when she thought she'd just about had enough, he'd move to another part of her body, her breasts or even her hands, to make love to her there until she wanted to bash him over the head to let her come again. Who knew that someone's hands could be such an erotic zone. Apparently, Robert did.

Then when he finally entered her, she came so many times that she lost count. And all he'd done was slide his cock into her heat, and that was all it took. The man was an artist. She bet that he'd even make a —

"Elizabeth? I've been calling your name for five

minutes." She smiled up at the woman. There was no way she could have remembered her name with all the lust that was running through her mind right now. "It's Carole from Admitting. You admitted Mr. Carson. I think that if you'd look at his chart, you'd see that he's not to be admitted unless it's just to keep him from dying."

"Why is that?" She told her that he owes the hospital a great deal of money from when his wife passed, and if he dies, the hospital will be eating all the money he still owes us. "You do know that you can't not treat a person for billing, right? It's a federal statute that states that."

"Yes, I'm aware of that. But we don't admit him. Ever. We only have to treat him in the emergency room, and that's the limit to the law." Elizabeth asked her what she was supposed to do with him if he needed more care. "I don't care. I only care that you can't admit him. I'll have to have you go and discharge him as soon as you can. Today before four so that he doesn't rack up another day of billing. He's taking up room that we don't need him to do. Not to mention time and money that another patient, a paying one, can use from us."

"I was having a really good day until you came to me. How much does he owe the hospital? I'm sure you have an exact amount right there on your chart." She told her. "Let me get this straight. You're not going to allow a man that is in his late seventies, who lost his wife a month ago, to sully your rooms up for ten grand? Christ woman, I have more than that in debt, well, I don't, but most people do. What do you expect him to do? Take out a bank loan that he won't be able to pay either so that he gets the treatment that he needs?"

"As I said before, I don't care." Elizabeth reached for her backpack, her usual mode of a purse and pulled out her credit card. "What are you doing? I hope you're not thinking of doing what I think you are."

"What does it look like I'm doing?" She told her what she thought. "Bing. Bing. Bing. You win the prize. Yes, I'm paying off his bill. Take this and pay it off, and then he might live another few years after the infection that is—where the hell are you going? You didn't take my card."

"I'm not going to either. I want you to discharge him this minute. Christ woman. What do you think will happen when everyone hears that if they're down on their luck, just call Doctor Elizabeth Archer, and she'll make your hospital bills—"

"What the hell is going on over here?" Not only did Darrel sit down, but Katie did as well. Elizbeth didn't think that Carole knew who Katie was. If she did, she didn't seem to care. Darrel looked around as he continued talking to Carole. "Keep your voice down. Do you want the hospital to think that there is trouble here?"

"There is." She huffed and sat down. "Your sister-in-law here just admitted Mr. Carson. I was just telling her that she has to discharge him because we don't have the money to be treating patients that are behind in their payments. Not to mention, he's going to die soon, and who will pick up the tab then? No one will. And we'll be out thousands of dollars that pays the dollars that go to your paychecks. Now she wants to pay it off. Like that's going to do a lot of good when he'll owe more when he's out of here or dead. Dead would be better. That way, we can claim it on our—"

"Shut your fucking mouth right now before I shut it for you." Elizabeth and Darrel looked at Katie. She was about as angry as she'd ever seen her. "You're fired."

"You can't fire me. I'm on the board of directors, and I'm the one that makes it so that we can keep the power on when no one else can." Katie looked at Darrel before standing up and pulling out her phone. Carole seemed to be on a high or something because she didn't stop. "The nerve of some people. Don't they have any idea how hard it is to keep money in the coffers for bonuses at the end of the year? I don't know who she thinks that she is, but she'll be wanting us to take care of her sometime soon—" she looked at Katie before speaking again. "I'm thinking not too long from now, and we'll have to turn her away because some degenerate will be taking up the last bed that had no more intentions of paying than I'm sure that she has."

"Do you know who she is?" Carole said she didn't but knew her to be a troublemaker like Elizabeth. Darrel shook his head. "Christ, you're in so much trouble right now. I only hope that you only lose your job and not your life over this. I've never seen her so upset before."

When Katie sat back down. She had the oddest smile on her face. While she still had her credit card out, she wondered if what Robert had told her was true. They didn't have a limit on it. But she was going to pay off the billing that Mr. Carson owed to this ridiculous place. She got up just as the police showed up.

"Hello, Katie." The captain of the police force kissed Katie on the cheek. "I'm to understand that you needed our help? I stopped by the security office, and they said that we can have the call. Something about the woman being a real tyrant."

"I'd like for you to arrest this woman. Also, I don't doubt that she is a tyrant. She actually wants my son and daughter-in-law to have poor old Mr. Carson taken home, and I know for a fact that he's still receiving treatment from Elizabeth here. Isn't it nice to have such caring doctors in the family?" Officer Bob, how he told Darrel to call him, shook his hand, then hers. "Now, I'll have to make a few phone calls after she's—"

"You can't have me arrested. What is wrong with you people today. Simply because I want a man out of here that isn't paying his bill? Get away from me before I have to report you to the board." Katie asked her if she knew who the board members were. "I don't know, but I'm sure that they're going to side with me on this."

"Doubtful anyone would side with you on anything, dear. Darrel, will you make arrangements to have Mr. Carson's—Oh, thank you, Elizabeth. Darrel, take this card down and pay off his bill, please. Even if it were to come to that, which I'm doubting before he's kicked to the side of the road." Before she could say much more, which actually didn't stop her, Carole was taken away in cuffs. "I'm going to have to let you two make sure that this doesn't happen again. To think of that poor man being—Well, we'll take care that it isn't going to happen again."

As Katie sat there, a cup of tea in a fancy tea cup, was brought to her as well as a piece of pie for the three of them. She was so polite to them it was hard for Elizabeth to wrap her head around the fact that the woman had actually said the word fuck. And had gotten someone taken away in cuffs. When Darrel left them to pay off the bill, she just stared at the older woman.

"You're not as soft as people think you are, are you, Katie Archer?" She just grinned at her. Elizabeth grinned back. "Also, and I might be wrong about this, but you can get all fired up when you need to as well. Are you on the board of directors of his hospital?"

"There is no longer a board of any kind here at this hospital. I run the place as of nine this morning. To think that they liked profit over making people feel better just burns my toast. I had heard. However, it was nice to be able to hear it firsthand that Carole was going around having people discharge patients right and left. Did you hear about the pregnant woman that had given birth to twins?" Elizabeth shook her head. "Well, she won't have any more trouble about getting pain medication when she needs it. Can you imagine telling a woman that just gave birth to two eight pound babies that her insurance wasn't going to pay for extras like things to make her feel better? If I had been in the room with her, I would have knocked Carole's socks off. My goodness. Robert was almost ten pounds and only one child, and I thought I'd given birth to a hippo. Don't tell him that, dear. I don't want him to get a complex about it."

Elizabeth couldn't help it. She let go of a burst of laughter that had people turning to look at her. Katie only smiled, and Elizabeth leaned over and kissed her on the cheek. She asked her what that was for.

"For being about the best thing that has ever come into my life since Robert. Are you going to help me when I have my baby?" She said that, of course, she would. "In June?"

"Well, I don't know why the date is so important to you, but I'll help you at any time that—" Katie looked at her hard. "Elizabeth, are you telling me that you're going to have a child with my boy?"

"He's not really a boy. I mean, Christ, he makes me scream every time we have sex. Thinking of him as a boy is kind of gross. Even from his mom. But yes, we're having a baby." Katie cried. "Please don't do that. Please. You're going to have me all emotional, then we'll be a sloppy mess when Darrel comes back with my credit card."

"He won't use yours. He'll use his own, but he'd not say anything to that terrible woman. Are you really going to have a baby?" Elizabeth nodded. "I'm so happy. More grandchildren to watch grow up. Robert must be over the moon about this."

"He is, but we've not told anyone yet. I wasn't even supposed to tell you. But you've made me so happy by getting rid of the bitch that I'd about do anything for you." They hugged and were still hugging when Darrel did return. He looked at them oddly but didn't ask. It seemed like that was the best way to do things in his family.

"I had Rosie find out who else had been on the verge of being discharged and paid them off as well. There wasn't all that much, not when you think about how many people we see daily." Katie told him he was a good boy. "Thank you, mother. I learned from the best. Also, it will please you to know that all the men and women in the billing department are thrilled to death that they don't have to hound those people anymore. I guess Carole had them calling them several times a day to get money. I think we can find a better use of their time than calling the elderly up hourly and telling them that they're dead beats."

"Did she really do that?" Peter handed them both a sheet of paper that had the things they were supposed to say to people to get them to pay their bills. Katie folded up her script and put it in her purse—her pocketbook is what she called it. "I'm going to show this to Del. My goodness, he'll have that woman in irons before the end of the day."

After Katie left them, giving them both a kiss on the cheek, Elizabeth finished her glass of water, and Darrel finished his meal. When he was finished, she asked him if he was all right. He shrugged at first, then smiled at her.

"I didn't use your card, even though I could have used it to pay off all the bills here, and Robert wouldn't have cared." She thanked him. "I would like for you and I to do just what mom said, to keep an eye on patients to see if they're suffering for fear of being kicked out. You and the staff in your department have a better angle on it than I do, so I'd appreciate it if you and your staff could keep an eye on that for us. There is no reason for people to feel pressured when all they want to do is feel better. We'll have a fundraiser for it sometime in the summer, and that will bring in enough to help cover costs when this happens again."

"Will people want to help others with their billing?" He told her that not only would they help, but with Del running for state rep, he'd get all kinds of people working on it with them. "Good. I can get on board with that. Also, you should know that I've been keeping an eye on a couple of things in the ER department. There are some things going on in there. While not bad, they are a little unprofessional. Were you aware that there is a great deal of stealing going on? Not huge things like equipment but scrubs. Scissors and tape. As I said, not huge, but I'm betting at least a million a year if you were to track all departments about it."

"I don't know that I care about that much money going out in their pockets." She asked him why not. "They come to work daily. Do, for the most part, a wonderful job when here. And I couldn't ask for a better staff than what I have on the floors that I have patients on. How about you?"

"I suppose you're right. But I will keep an eye on it. I don't think you or anyone else will be happy if we just stop looking at the bottom line when it comes to that." He told her thanks. "For what? I've just told you that we're losing money on some of the employees."

"Yes, you did. But you came to me and not to someone like Carole. I love you, Elizabeth, as much as my brothers. You and I are going to make this place a place that people can come to for comfort as well as feeling better too."

When he left her, she gathered her things up to go back to work. It wasn't as if she wanted to go home now. Robert had already told her that he was working late to get the room he'd been working on inspected. If she went home now, she'd just be bored and eat dinner without him. And she loved him too much to do that.

Chapter 7

Robert read over the agreement three times just to be sure he was getting it right. The agreement between Avery and Lance wasn't complicated, but it was too. She wasn't taking the building, which Lance had a buyer for, but she was taking all the contents of the building. Also, and this one he'd not thought of, she was to receive all the money from the sale of the items in the building, even any and all items made by his sister. That scared him a little. He was sure that the dresses or whatever she sold would be worth more now that the young woman had been murdered and her murderers captured in such a big headline way. But Lance wanted nothing to do with them. Not because he didn't love his sister, but because he was paving a new life for himself, and he needed to not dwell on what might have been if Lannie hadn't been murdered.

Lance wanted it done this way and didn't care about the profits. Robert was also taking care of the insurance money that was to come to him as well as any other money that came to him as formal payment from the municipals around the state. There was quite a bit of that as well.

"I don't really need the money. Our parents, as terrible as they were, left us well off. Millions and millions of dollars. I could never work again—which I will do—and never have to worry about where my next meal is coming from."

So Robert had been asked to take care of things for him while he was gone. Even going so far as to have his things moved from his home to the place he was in the process of buying close to downtown. While he was gone, Lance was going to give serious thought to becoming a member of the police force. But not the captain. He said that wasn't for him.

When Robert looked up from his work, Sherman was sitting there with his head back and his eyes closed. Not bothering to wake him, he leaned back in his own chair and decided that his brother had the right idea. Napping sounded good. But just as he was getting his body to relax, William startled awake. Robert asked him if he was all right.

"Yes. Just not sleeping well. I have something I'd like to talk to you about. I've been thinking about going back to school. Not as a student but as a teacher. I would like to teach younger kids. Try to form them into something more than the little shits that I see when I'm around a bigger city." Robert asked him why he needed to talk to him about that. For him to just do it. "I thought you'd say that, but it's more than that. I don't want to come off as a know-it-all when I don't even have children of my own. So, last week I volunteered at the grade school to see if I could handle a bunch of kids. It wasn't nearly as bad as I thought it would be."

Robert laughed. "I'm sorry. But what did you expect? Them to be little monsters that bite and spit at people?"

"I honestly didn't know what to expect. I've been hanging around Del's kids, who I love, and they seem normal enough. But really, they're not. I don't mean that they're mean or anything, but most kids aren't as well adjusted as you'd think they are. For what they grew up with and the things that they had to endure. The kids at the grade school were curious little people with a great sense of their surroundings. I'm not sure I'm staying this right." Robert said that he didn't understand. "There was this one boy, Clay, that is obviously coming from a fucked up home life. Most of the time, he doesn't have anything to eat. And even though he would more than likely qualify for free meals, he said that his dad won't let him do that because he'd lose some of the money on their food card. I looked it up, and it doesn't affect that card at all. Also, he said that they never have food in the house."

"What did you do, Sherman? I have a feeling that I'm going to have to be representing you in some kind of kidnapping thing." He said that he'd not do that. "But you're thinking about it."

"Sort of. I've called social services on the dad. I'm not sure how long it will take them to take care of this, but Clay is going to end up starving to death if someone doesn't step in and take care of the situation that he's in through no fault of his own." He asked him what he needed from him. "If it comes to it, I'd like to take him in as a primary caregiver. I guess I'd like to be a host to children that need a safe place to stay while things are being taken care of for them. Foster care seems like a stupid name for something that will be the very life or death of some kids, but that's what I want to do. To help kids in a way that otherwise might not be open to them."

"I like that idea. What is it you need for me to do for you?" He told him what he needed. "I don't think you'll have any trouble, but yes, I'll help you out with all the necessary paperwork. But you're an attorney too. Why not do it yourself?"

"I don't want anyone to say that I fucked around with my own paperwork. Everyone that knows you, knows that you'd do the right thing no matter who you were representing." He wasn't sure what he meant but didn't ask. It sounded like he was saying he'd feed him to the wolves if it came to it. "Mom doesn't know. I know for a fact that she'd just move in and make it happen by just calling in a few favors or something. I love her to pieces, but I believe she'd make this happen so that I can be happy. And this does make me feel really happy. Happier than I've been in a long while, Robert."

"Then I'm on board too. However, if mom finds out you're doing this and you didn't ask her for some kind of help, she'll be hurt. I mean, even if they're only with you temporarily, she'll adopt them as her grandchildren. You know that, don't you?" Sherman said he hadn't thought of that. "I'll do this for you because I think it's a wonderful idea, but you need to tell mom. If not, then she'll find out somehow and will be all the more hurt from it because you didn't tell her."

"You're right. I never thought of that. I might need her help anyway. She has a way of getting things I wouldn't have thought of until it was too late. Like clothing they might need. Extra plates and such." Robert named a few other things that he might have an issue with. "All right. As soon as I leave here, I'm going to go and talk to her. To be honest, that never occurred to me. I know that children are sexually abused, I ran into it a great deal as an attorney, but I hadn't thought of their reaction to me giving them a bath. All right. I'm going to hire a full-time nurse too. I'll have Darrel and Elizabeth see what they can do for me in that respect."

After Sherman left, about as excited as he'd seen him in a while, he began looking up things that would be required for his brother to become a foster parent. Or, as he said, a temporary safe place for kids to be able to be safe and fed. It looked like he was pretty much on the way to being able to hit all the requirements for it other than a couple of minor things that would be easy to take care of. Having a nearly endless supply of money would help a great deal. With two dependable doctors in the family would be a plus for him as well.

When he had all the information he could find and some notes to go over with William, he finished what he was doing for Avery and went to the job site. They'd asked him not to come to his home anymore. He was driving them crazy by asking questions. And since he and Elizabeth wanted the house done soon, he was to stay away and stop making them insane. Smiling, he made his way to the job site that they'd only just started today.

It was a total kitchen remodel. As soon as he entered the house, he felt a sense of warmth. Tearing out the kitchen to the studs wasn't something that he'd do, but then it wasn't his home. The house itself was older and full of charm. But the kitchen was going to be modern. There would be every gadget known to man in it because the people were entertainers. Whatever the hell that meant nowadays.

Bingo was sitting at a makeshift table watching the men put up drywall. It was something that he enjoyed, so Robert sat with him. Bingo simply looked over and smiled at him before turning back to the job in front of them.

"I have another job for you should you want to take it on." Robert reminded him that they were partners. "I know that, but this is a big job. Not huge, but bigger than anything we've done in a while. It's a build. From the ground being readied to the finished home. I've not had the occasion to do one from the ground up for a while now."

"I've no idea where to even start on one of those." Bingo nodded, watching the drywall go up. "What is it you're not telling me about this new build?"

"I'm going to be the homeowner. I just want me something that I can play around in. A couple of bedrooms, not including my own. Warm floors that don't freeze up my feet when I get up in the middle of the night. Something that maybe a great grandkid or two might be coming over to spend the night. I want me a pool too with a cover in the winter so I can keep it warm for myself and the kids." He finally looked at him. "I've been thinking about a couple of things for it too that I think you might be able to get on board with. I want solar panels all over the roof. In the back yard too, if we can manage it. A garden of my own so that I can go out and pick me some green beans when I want them. A greenhouse off the back if that's possible."

"You want a house that is green, I'm assuming." He nodded, then watched the drywallers. "Bingo, there's more to this than that. Something is wrong. I have no idea what it might be, but there is something that you're not telling me, isn't there?"

"I went to the doctor today. Well, last week, too, but he did one of them biopsy things on me. I got me some cancer." Robert felt his eyes fill with tears at the thought of losing this old man. "I've not told Elizabeth. Not yet. I will, but I'm working up to it. Now, don't be going to her about it. I need to deal with it on my own. But I want to make sure that I leave something behind that will say that I was here. Something that makes people say that old Bingo, he was a hell of a man."

"I don't know if you realize this or not, but I believe people say that about you now, old man." He laughed a little, as did Bingo. "Where is it, and is there anything we can do about it to keep you around a little longer. I wasn't supposed to say anything, but Elizabeth is going to have a baby in June."

He turned to look at him so quickly that Robert heard his neck pop. Asking him if he was kidding an old man, Robert assured him that he'd never joke to him about a baby coming. Patting him on the hand, he turned back to the men working.

"It's in my kidney. Left one. It's just a small spot right now, but it could spread if I don't have surgery now. I don't want to. I'm an old man, and to know that I'd have to go under a knife at my age, well, it scares me more than I can say. I'll need me a place to recoup. I'm assuming you won't mind me being all tuckered out at your house." Robert told him he was welcome forever if he wanted to be. "I need my own space. That's the reason for the house. When I come out of the recouping stage, I'm going to need me a place to get some peace and quiet. You know as well as I do that Elizabeth is going to pepper me to death in making sure I'm all right. I have to talk to her, I know that, but I have to deal with it on my own for a little bit longer. It just seemed right to tell you. Like you'd not be asking questions that I don't remember the answers to right now."

"The next time you go to the doctor, you should take my brother with you. Or my grandda. At one time, I think he was a mediator of sorts when people went to the doctor for bad news or whatever, and he'd be there to dumb it down for them. Not that I think that's your problem, but I'm thinking that after he said that it was cancer, you didn't hear another word." He said that was what happened. "My grandda would love to be there for you. You and he seem to get along well enough for that."

"He's my friend, and I should have taken him when I talked to the doctor this morning. It's a terrible thing to live to be as old as I am only to find out that now that you've reached an age where you feel like you can take it easy, cancer comes along and bites you in the butt." Robert had to look away himself. He loved this old man as much as he did his own grandda. "You don't go on about this, young man. I'm not dead yet. I have a lot of things that I can still teach you."

"You're damned right you have." They sat there in silence. Robert was thinking about not being able to just come to see Bingo when he wanted. And how hard Elizabeth was going to take this. For as hard as he was taking this, she was going to be ten times worse with it. "Would you like me to be there when you tell Elizabeth? I will. You just tell me when and I'll be there with you."

"Nah, but I do thank you. I think this is something that I need to do on my own. I won't be able to ease up with it with her. She'll pound me on the head if I try that stuff with her. She's a good girl, that one, but she can be hard on a person that pussy foots around with her." They both laughed again. "I thank you for telling me about the baby, Robert. I won't give it away that you told me. She'll tell me when I talk to her. Just to keep it out there that I have something to look forward to."

Bingo left him shortly after that. They hugged tightly, the two of them, then he left. Robert had to go out on the deck to gather his emotions before he could set to work. Today was going to take all his concentration, and he didn't want to have to worry about thinking of the wrong thing at the wrong time. Putting in tile would, he hoped, keep him from sobbing in his soup as his grandda says all the time.

~*~

Elizabeth wasn't sure what to say to her grandda. He'd come into the house about an hour ago, told her he had cancer, what his plans were regarding it, then sat down and turned on the television. Like she was going to sit there with him and watch a preseason football game with him. Taking the remote from him, she knew he'd not been paying attention when she turned it off, and he turned to look at her with tears in his eyes.

"I thought for sure you didn't care what I just said to you." She kissed him on the cheek and then smacked him in the same place. "What was that for?"

"For thinking that I'd not care about you. You old

goat. What did you think was going to happen when you told me this? And you'd better be around for my baby when it comes. I'll never forgive you if you're not here." He nodded, then looked at her strangely. "I know, you know. I haven't any idea how you found out, but you've been glancing at my belly ever since you arrived. And pampering me. You know that I hate that."

"Robert told me. I promised him that I'd not tell you, but you're just too darn smart for me to pull the wool over your eyes. I'm an old man. Next time you think about smacking me around, remember that I spanked your bottom when you were a baby." She told him he'd never hit her. "Will you just let me fib a little? No, I didn't spank you. Not that you didn't need it once in a while, but no, I didn't. I've been making arrangements about this cancer business. I'm going to do everything that I'm supposed to do and then some. Robert is going to help me get a house that I can live in when you get to pestering me too much. And you will. You have to know that."

"Yes. I will. I'll try not to, but I'll not be able to help myself. But I don't want you to move out." He said that he did need his own space and that Robert needed to learn how to build a home. "I suppose he does. But where are you going to be living? Not far, I'm hoping."

"No, not far but not close either. You're already pestering me, and I've not even done a darned thing yet." She moved closer to him and hugged him. "I'll be just fine and dandy, child. I'm an old man, and it's about my time anyway. This way, I can plan things better instead of living by the seat of my butt all the time. I'm going to stop and smell them darned roses that your grannie used to tell me about all the time."

"Grandda, I can't lose you. You're my heart." He said that the new baby would take up his space and that Robert would love her until she died. "He will, and so will the baby, but there isn't any way that a baby will be able to fill out my heart for the love that I have for you."

"You're a good girl, Elizabeth. The best there is. But I was going to die anyway. This way, as I said, I can give myself a little time to get used to it. I've not thought of it since you come home from college telling me that you were accepted in that doctor program." Elizabeth kissed him again. "There you go. Just what this old man needed. Some loving from his best granddaughter."

She held him until he got up to move. He'd been like that her entire life. Unable to sit for too long before his body just had to move. When he stared out the window at the yard, she asked him if he was really all right. His nod was all she got in regard to him answering her.

"Grandda, I'd like to go with you to the doctor. Or at least speak to him. I won't browbeat you into allowing me to go, but I'd like a better understanding of what you're up against." He said that he'd rather she wait for a bit, but she could call him. "I'll do that. What is his plan for treatment? Did he explain that to you?"

"He might have, but after—Robert said this to me—after I heard the word cancer, I didn't hear another thing that I can put my finger on. He might well have told me that I have won the lottery, but I'd of not heard it. I'm taking Del with me the next time. He'll listen to him, then when I have questions, he'll know how to tell me without telling me too much. You'd be good at the listening part, but I just need to ease into this for now. Do you understand?" She said that she did. That she'd more than likely make him more confused with her questions. "You might well at that. Robert said that Del has done this a few times, gone in with people so that they can get answers when they have time to get their mind settled. Mine ain't settled just yet. I'm getting there, but it's all jumbled up with things that are still circling around in my head."

"I can understand that. I really can." He nodded.

"Grandda, I love you. So much. If you need anything from me, you only have to ask me. I'll move heaven and earth for you."

"I know that. I surely do, but this is something that I have to deal with on my own for a bit. Not that I don't need help now and in the future, but I don't need to get into things that I just ain't ready to deal with just yet." Again she understood that but didn't push him into answering questions that she did have. "I'm going to do everything I'm told. I know that I said that before but I'm going to be taking good care of myself and getting the treatment that—he did say that I could have as many as five or ten years left if I do things right. That doesn't mean anything, however, if the cancer comes back. But he said that chances are good and that I'm going to be all right. You forget words like that when you're sitting there counting down the days until you think you're a dead man."

"I know something right now. I'm going to be a better person that needs to tell people bad news from now on." He said that he'd not meant to make her feel terrible about her and him. "No, you're absolutely right. I would have driven you over the edge about things that you're a grown man and will be able to take care of on your own. However, I can also see this from the side of a doctor. I wonder how many times I've told someone about their family member dying or is going to die, and they've not heard a single word I've said to them after that. I want to be more compassionate. More of a doctor that cares that they understand what I'm telling them."

"Well, if that's all that comes out of this, then I'm happy for it. There are a few things that I might have to come to you about to be dumbed down to me. Sometimes doctors do that too. Think that since you're looking at them, you understand the gobbly-goop they're telling you. While I think of myself as a smart man, there are terms they use, just on account of them using them all the time, that I don't get. I know enough to ask about them, but like this time, I had other things on my mind than what kind of Chemo he was talking about. To be honest, I didn't know there were different kinds of it."

"There are, Grandda, and if you'll allow me to, I'll be happy to dumb down whatever gobbly-goop you need." She got up and hugged him, then stepped back so as not to crowd him. "You're my hero. You've taken this news and turned it around for me in such a way that I feel better about the treatment that you're getting. Not only that, but I think I might just learn a thing or two while I'm at it."

Moving off the subject, they talked about the baby. He was telling her about some of the things that had been stored in the attic of this old house and that she should have Robert and his brothers bring down. Not only were there clothes that her grandmother had made for her and her mother before her, but also things like a rocker, bed, and, he thought, a dresser. Whatever was up there, she was going to use it. Simply to bring the feeling of homeness to the house and baby's room.

She and her grandda started dinner. While she could cook, it wasn't one of her favorite things to do. But he wanted meatloaf like grannie used to make, so she followed the recipe that he gave her, and it smelled wonderful as it baked for them. Making mashed potatoes, her favorite food and green beans were wonderful smells as well, and grandda made a batch of homemade rolls that would 'sop' up the gravy when it was finished cooking.

"And if there is any leftovers, these babies will make wonderful cold meatloaf sammiches." Not being a fan of hot meatloaf, she couldn't imagine having one of them cold on a bun. But this was his night, and she was going to do whatever he wanted. Katie even brought over some macaroni salad that she'd made too much of for their dinner. By the time Robert made it home, dinner was ready to be served, and she was happy that he seemed to enjoy it as much as grandda did.

Having a nice fire in the fire pit that had been built that day, the three of them made smores and had hot cocoa to drink. It wasn't terribly cold out yet, but it was the best fun she'd had in a while. Robert loved chocolate, so he would use twice as many chocolate bars, and grandda didn't care for marshmallows all that much, so he'd cut them in half and only cook part of one.

Going up to bed, she told Robert about the things in the attic and how she wanted to get them down soon. Even if they didn't use them right away for the baby, she did want to get them cleaned up and ready to go. He was, between yawns telling her that he knew someone that could clean them up for them and that he'd repaint them if necessary. Before she came out of the bathroom where she'd put on her nightgown, he was fast asleep, lying half in and on the bed. She really did love this man. More than she thought that he knew.

Chapter 8

There was no hope for it. Tally was going to have to go to Ohio and figure out what the fuck was going on with her brother. The fucker. He'd better be sick or dead, or she was going to get his ass in trouble again. All he had to do was tell her Clay was doing all right in school and send her a list of things he needed for winter. She'd buy them, never sending him money, then send them on to him.

Tally had been afraid that he was selling the things off instead of giving them to her nephew. Since Allice had left Howie, he'd been using more. Not that she thought he'd ever stopped, but he had some way of getting around Social Services when they'd show up at his house when she called.

Letting the phone ring and ring, she tried to remember when the last time she'd been to see Howie. It had to be at least a month now. The bastard had made her stay in a hotel rather than letting her bunk on the couch in order to see the little boy who had come to mean the world to her.

"What the fuck do you want?" She wasn't bothered by his tone anymore. It didn't even bother her that he sounded drunk. Recording each and every call to and from him was something that the internet told her that she should do. "Tally, I'm busy. What the fuck are you doing calling me when I know for a fucking fact that you can't afford to miss a day of work. You should be at work right now. My rent is coming due."

"I'm not working right now." She sat down while he began screaming at her about his money. "Shut the fuck up." That seemed to get his attention.

"What do you mean you're not working? You'd better be. I'm telling you right now if I don't have rent money from you, I'm going to sell off this fucking kid. He's not worth spit as it is now. Just last week, I had to go into a meeting with the school because he wasn't bringing himself any lunch in to eat." She asked him if he'd packed him something. "No. Why should I have to get him something to eat to take to school? He's old enough to know what he'll eat or not."

"He's six, Howie. I don't think I should have to point that out to you that a six year old doesn't know that he's supposed to hit all the food groups when making his lunch. Why the hell aren't you making it for him?" He said that he wasn't getting up that early. "Then make it the night before. Though I don't know why you're not getting up to put him on the bus in the first place. Why aren't you?"

"Ain't none of your bees wax. Get off my back. When are you going to be sending the money for my rent, Tally? I'm telling you right now, I won't put up with you delaying it again. You know that I'm serious about selling him off?" While she was glad that he was saying these things for the recording, she wasn't happy to know that he would do just what he said he would again. "I need that five hundred dollars pronto."

"Your rent isn't that much. It's only one-fifty because you live in a government-subsidized housing. Which you said you didn't. And you don't pay any utilities like you told me, either. I've been doing some research, Howie. Nothing you've said to me is true." He didn't say anything. "What have you been doing with the money that I've been sending you? I was also informed that the school will supply him with a free meal if you were to go in and fill out the paperwork for it. Why haven't you done that either?"

"I was told that it would affect my food card." She hadn't realized that he was getting a food card either. It never occurred to her that he'd lie to her about so many things. "With me and little Howie here, we get a nice size of money that can fill the fridge up a few times a month. But it won't go as far if I have to go in there and tell them to give him some food when I ain't got anymore left for him. He don't eat much anyway. And don't think that I didn't notice that you didn't tell me why you're not working. I want that money, Tally. I deserve it for having to be around this kid all day."

"He's a good kid, and I doubt very much he wants to be around you either, Howie. Will you stop calling him little Howie? His name is Clayton. There isn't any reason whatsoever that you call him that." Howie told her that Beth should have named him after her. "She should have kicked your sorry ass to the side of the road when you went to prison for robbery. The very fact that she put your name on his birth certificate at all is a surprise to me. You're nothing but crap. Where is Clay? I want to talk to him."

"Not unless you have some money for me, you're not." She cried then, careful not to show her brother how much his words hurt her. "You're not working. Why the fuck not?"

"A big company bought the place and is tearing the building down to put in a parking lot. I guess they think that a little grocery store isn't as important as having people have a place to park." She wanted to scream about how it wasn't her fault that the building was as old as rocks.

It leaked like there wasn't a roof on it when it only rained a little. The furnace was temperamental, as in it would only work if you begged it to work. There was no air in the place, but up front, when you first came in and all that came from a window air conditioner. The freezers had given out about a year ago, so they no longer had ice cream. Meats were all right, she supposed, but that fridge was going out as well. Well, it did go out the day that the new company that owned the building came in. Christ, she didn't know what she was going to do now.

With paying her brother a thousand dollars a month when she didn't have to was killing her on top of her own bills. If she never ate another peanut butter and jelly sandwich, she'd be happy. Also, ramen noodles. Tally had a list of things that she could do with them longer than she thought most people had thought of. All just so she could save her nephew from being sold off like Howie threatened to do weekly. It was then that she realized that he'd hung up on her.

When Beth had left Howie, no one believed her when she told the police that she thought he'd killed her, the baby was left behind. Beth would never have left that little boy, and when she did leave, she would have come to her and told her that she was leaving. But Howie had won that battle, and he'd been stuck, his words having to care for a little baby all on his own. She'd gone to help him for a while, staying in a hotel that she could ill afford after buying diapers, formula and other items that Clay had needed.

But it only lasted for the first couple of months before she had to return to her work. Each day she would care for Clay while Howie did whatever he did during the day and at night, she'd hunt for clues that would tell her where Beth was. She'd been close, she thought, when Howie had caught her looking around. Christ, she'd barely made it home with all her injuries after the beating that she'd taken that day.

After that, he'd forbidden her to come around. But it didn't stop her from having to send him money. Then she'd found out, quite by accident, that Howie was getting not just a food card but insurance, subsidized rent for housing.

Going to her cot, not even the size of a twin bed, she laid down on it to try and rest. Tomorrow she was going to have to find a job, or she'd not even have this wreck of a place to live. When the couple next door started their nightly fight, she got down off the cot and hid under it. There were always guns involved in their kind of nightly ritual.

The knock at her door sometime later woke her up from a nightmarish sort of dream. It was nearly always the same. Beth begging her not to tell her brother that she was having a son, him finding out and chasing her all over the place with a gun. Staggering to the door, she opened it without looking.

"You didn't even ask who it was. For all you knew, I could have been a murderer. Or came here to rob you." She slammed the door in his face and went to the bathroom. She could hear him pounding on the doors when she went back to her cot to lie down again. "Open the fucking door. I don't want to be here anymore than you want to talk to me. It's about the place you used to work. I have a check here for you to help you get along until you find another job."

"Fuck you. If you'd just left the place alone, I'd still have a job, and I wouldn't have to be wondering where my next meal is coming from." She did get up, curious about the check, had her opening the door and taking the envelope from the big man. Tally was ready to slam the door in his face again when he put his foot in the door. The couple took that opportunity to start firing at each other again, and she knocked the man back when one of the bullets went by her nose. When the guns were finished, she sat up and looked at the man beneath her. He had his eyes closed, so she smacked him around — which actually felt pretty good, considering. He looked at her with one eye.

"You're bleeding." She shrugged at him. "You were shot. Is this something that you have to put up with all the time?"

"No, I only stay in this house in the winter months. My summer home is much more bullet-riddled. I've been shot before. If you don't have anything else to impart to me, I'd like to get back to what I was doing."

"Plotting the deaths of other people?" She moved off of him, making sure that she elbowed him at least four times before she was on her feet. "You're really bleeding a great deal. I'm going to call an ambulance."

"Well, I hope you get in it on your own because I'm not going to be able to pay the seven hundred bucks they'll charge me for not taking it to the hospital. That is, if they show at all. This isn't exactly the best of neighborhoods in the event that you didn't know that." She looked at the blood on her blouse and then put her hand over the wound. It hurt like hell, but she wasn't going to go anywhere. "What else did you want to tell me? That you're all making it so that we don't have to look for jobs? That there is one that is providing transportation as well? Go home, whoever the hell you are and have a nice life."

She did get to slam the door in his face this time as he'd sat up enough so that she could do that. When her neighbors started screaming about her making all that noise, she didn't bother speaking to them. They'd just fire into her room again, and she didn't have time for that shit. Going to the bathroom again, she pulled out her dwindling first aid kit and looked at what she had to deal with.

The man must have left because when she went out of her place to go downstairs to get her milk and eggs, the snow had already covered his prints leaving the building to a parking lot. Getting her things out of the snow that had piled up overnight, she was glad now that she'd been able to get some food the day before. Otherwise, she'd be shit out of luck in getting out now. Taking it into the house to cook, she was suddenly not all that hungry. Her wound was bleeding badly now, and she wasn't sure that she shouldn't at least call someone to fix it for her.

The only doctor that she knew was the vet that lived below her. Well, he wasn't a vet any longer. He'd lost his license some time ago when he'd been doing illegal things to the poor animals left in his care. Tally never asked, but she had a feeling that it wasn't just cutting them up but sexual things too. Shivering, she put her things out the window onto the little deck — that was too dangerous to hold a plant and warmed herself up in her cot.

Sleeping fitfully, she had strange dreams about shit that she didn't know what it meant. There was a woman in white that was standing over her, yelling at the man that had been at the door. Police had come in and were taking away her neighbors. An elderly woman, a very beautiful one at that, was asking her why she was living here, and she did remember answering her. What she said, Tally had no idea, but she must have said something because she, too, disappeared.

"Don't leave my milk outside. It'll freeze up, and I won't have any hot cocoa in the morning." Someone asked her if she had any coffee. "Who the hell can afford coffee? I can barely buy a candy bar to melt down for my cocoa once a month after sending my deadbeat brother everything I have. He'd better not be selling off Clay again. I'll murder his ass if he does that again."

She remembered some questions about her health and had no idea if she had answered them. It was the strangest dream that she'd ever had. When something warm, like a big old warm fuzzy blanket that she would get from her mom every Christmas seemed to float over her, she let herself dream about something else. Sometimes the past would come up and kick her in the ass so hard that she'd want to just starve herself to death rather than deal with it.

"It might be cheaper for me to just die, I think."

~*~

"If you don't calm your ass down, I'm going to

knock you back on it and see where that gets you. I said that I'd tell you what I knew, but I won't be bullied into giving you answers that I don't have. Sit down and shut the fuck up, William, or so help me, I'm going to call mom." William looked around as if mom might pop out of one of the rooms he was surrounded by. "Are you ready to listen or not?" Darrel would just walk away from him without giving him any answers. So he told him that he was ready. "All right. She's dehydrated, undernourished and has been shot before. The bullet, this time, only hit her belly, where we had to remove a portion of her colon to get it back to rights. The other bullets, two different times, were removed as well. One was lodged into her ribs the other was in her thigh. How she was able to get around after that one is—keep your mouth closed, or I will walk."

"Why the hell didn't she get help?" He didn't answer him. Anyone that had been in her apartment or really a room the size of a closet would know that she was barely making ends meet. "I offered to call her an ambulance to go in."

"Were you like this? All pissy and in a shitty mood. I don't know that I would have taken you up on it, either. But she was right in telling you that they might not have shown. There are records that indicate that one of her neighbors had died when it took them three days to get there to offer treatment. She might well have only survived before because she's not stupid enough to think anyone is going to help her. Which brings me to the question as to why you did. You don't seem to like anyone anymore, much less people that might want to depend on you. Even mom has been avoiding you."

"One of these women might be something to me, and I don't need a wife in my life. I think I like things just the way they are." Darrel pointed out that his disposition might keep the most determined away. "Don't be a jackass. I'm not in the mood."

After punching his brother in the face and walking away, knocking him back on his ass, Darrel went to recovery where Tally Washer was. She was doing well, considering she needed about thirty more pounds on her already slender body. When he went to the nurses' station to make sure they knew she was to have the best of care, Elizabeth was there waiting for him.

"She all right?" Darrel told her everything that he'd said to William and more. "I've had Del and Katie look into this brother of hers. I have a feeling that William knows who the kid is. He was just talking to Robert about him yesterday."

"Do you think that he really sold the kid off?" Elizabeth didn't say anything, which was saying volumes for her. "I see. So you believe this. Also, I heard from one of the nurses that Beth Washer is missing and presumed dead. What can you tell me about that?"

"Nothing. I did tell Del about it, and he's pulling some strings to find out. If he, Howard, killed her, then the little boy would be safer with Tally. That's her name, too, by the way. Not short for anything." They moved down the hall to the office he used when he was working here. "Tally had a job up until the store that she was working in was closed down. I guess that the land was bought by the family. And the store, after inspecting it, didn't even hit any of the code parameters for being a store. No heat, no air. The refrigerators were more than thirty years old and barely working. They had coolers out with bagged ice in them for the customers to sort through when they wanted something."

"Christ." She asked him if he wanted it all. "I don't think I want to know any more about that. Not right now, anyway. What about her story about the brother taking her money? I'm sure you have something on that by now."

"He apparently told her that his rent was too much for him to get around. Also, she supplied them with food and other items. Buying them first and then sending them to him so he'd not have the money. I don't know why he'd fuck over his sister like that, but some people just need to be killed. Howard didn't work but stayed at home all day. I don't even want to think about what the house might look like when there isn't an inspection slated for him to come in. He hires a group to come in and give the house a good cleaning so he can live there without any trouble. You'd think he'd be using that money on things for himself or Clay. Anyway, that's what I know. Oh, Clay has been picked up from school by Social Services and is on his way into the hospital to be looked over. I thought you or I should do it, but the police told me that they didn't want us going to the house to kill him if there was a nail cracked or something. I'd like to think I have a better hold on my temper than that." He just stared at her. "All right, I would have. But I'm telling you right now, I want to adopt that kid. He seems like he's been abused enough for someone so young."

"I don't know yet, but I believe you." She asked him about Tally. "She's going to be all right. It's going to take her a few days of her resting before I'd be happy with her being released. But where she'll go after that is beyond me. The complex where she was living has been condemned, and they're finding places for people that are there. I'm sure she could be on that list, too, but I didn't put her on it yet. I wanted to see if there were other takers for her that could keep an eye on her."

"You know that I'd love to do it." Darrel thanked her. "You're welcome. All right, I need to get my ass home and put my feet up. Then I have rotations with you tomorrow morning. Are we still up for that?"

"Yes. I can't thank you enough for helping my practice out while I take this trip. I've not had a vacation since I got out of college. I need it." She told him it was her pleasure. "When the baby comes along, I'll be there for you too."

"I know that all of you will be." The nurse said there was a call for Darrel and Elizabeth told him she'd talk to him later. "I'll be home if you need anything from me. I'm going to be working with the others on finding out some information about this family."

After saying his name in the phone, he had to pull it away from his ear so that he wouldn't damage his ear drum. Whoever was on the other end was not a happy person with him. As soon as the man took a breath to no doubt start on him again, Darrel whistled. That got his attention.

"Now, calmly tell me what the hell you're going on about so that I can understand. I don't have a clue what it is you're screaming at me about." He said that his name was Howie Washer. "All right. I know who you are. What do you want?"

"Someone told me that you took my kid from me. I'm going to make sure that I own your wallet before the end of the day." He said that he'd had nothing to do with his son being taken out of school. "Then who is it I have to murder to get him back. That kid is my ticket to a lot of things. One of them getting my sister in line with my stuff."

"You mean your sister, Tally Washer?" He asked him how he knew her name. "She's here at the hospital as well. She's been shot. Not for the first time, either, it seems."

"Well hell. How is she supposed to pay me if she's lazing around the hospital? You fix her up good enough that she can get out and get herself a job. I have things to pay off." He asked him why he didn't have a job. "I have a kid to watch over. Didn't you hear me saying that?"

"I heard you, but I doubt very much that you

watch him all that well. From the report I've gotten, he's barely eaten in a few days. Not to mention has anything to keep his feet warm in the winter." He told him that was Tally's job. While Darrel didn't have any reports yet, he could guess. "Why is that? You said he was your kid. Why is your sister paying for his things?"

"So I keep him." That sent a chill so far down his back that he was sure he'd feel it for a week or two. "I got to find out where I can find my kid. You know anything about him, you call me. I don't deserve to be treated like this. I might just have to come down there and hassle Tally some to find out what she's done now."

Darrel hung up the phone and then made a decision. "I don't want anyone to be able to come in and see Tally Washer unless it's my family. Nurses that you trust too." Nurse Able said her son would come in and guard her door. "I don't want anyone to get into trouble. Just make sure that no one goes in there without permission. I'll tell the front desk too."

"I'll take care of the desk downstairs. I'll even tell them that you said no information either. That'll keep his butt out of here. And Jeremiah won't get in a bit of trouble. He's a bouncer for that bar in Columbus that's so popular. I'll just say that I know her brother and that

I don't want any trouble for my staff. If anyone says anything, I'll have them talk to your momma. She'll be on my side."

She would be, indeed. After checking on Tally again, Darrell made his way home. He'd been working a lot of shifts lately and was looking forward to going on his trip. He'd not been skiing since he'd been in his last year of med school and was looking forward to it more than he could imagine. Not only that, but he was hoping to get laid once or twice. It couldn't hurt him to be a little relaxed once in a while.

Before You Go...

HELP AN AUTHOR

write a review

THANK YOU!

Share your voice and help guide other readers to these wonderful books. Even if it's only a line or two, your reviews help readers discover the author's books so they can continue creating stories that you'll love. Log in to your favorite retailer and leave a review. Thank you.

AWARD WINNING, BESTSELLING AUTHOR

Kathi Barton, a winner of the Pinnacle Book Achievement Award and a best-selling author on Amazon and All Romance books, lives in Nashport, Ohio, with her husband, Paul. When not creating new worlds and romance, Kathi and her husband enjoy camping and going to auctions. She can also be seen at county fairs with her husband, an artist and potter.

Her muse, a cross between Jimmy Stewart and Hugh Jackman, brings her stories to life for her readers in a way that has them coming back time and again for more. Her favorite genre is paranormal romance, with a great deal of spice. You can visit Kathi on line and drop her an email if you'd like. She loves hearing from her fans. aaronskiss@gmail.com.

Follow Kathi on her blog: http://kathisbartonauthor.blogspot.com/

www.ingramcontent.com/pod-product-compliance
Lightning Source LLC
Chambersburg PA
CBHW020621180626
46810CB00007B/2885